Journey to th...

WHAT ALSO MIGHT
BE MOUNTAINS

N

W

E

S

BORDERLANDS

THE RUINS

BIG HOLLOW
TREE

BIG YELLOW THREE

THE RUINS

TREE
HOUSE

MEETING HOUSE

GROVE

TAG'S HOUSE

THREE BIG PINES

FOREST

Windswept

Windswept

MARGI PREUS

Illustrated by ARMANDO VEVE

AMULET BOOKS • NEW YORK

The illustration for the jacket was made using graphite on paper with layers of digital color applied with Procreate and Photoshop. The interiors are graphite and ink on paper.

Cataloging-in-Publication Data has been applied for and may be obtained from the Library of Congress.

ISBN 978-1-4197-5824-9

Text © 2022 Margi Preus
Cover and interior illustrations © 2022 Armando Veve
Edited by Howard W. Reeves
Book design by Chelsea Hunter

Printed and bound in U.S.A.
10 9 8 7 6 5 4 3 2 1

Amulet Books are available at special discounts when purchased in quantity for premiums and promotions as well as fundraising or educational use. Special editions can also be created to specification. For details, contact specialsales@abramsbooks.com or the address below.

Amulet Books® is a registered trademark of Harry N. Abrams, Inc.

ABRAMS The Art of Books
195 Broadway, New York, NY 10007
abramsbooks.com

To all readers, present and future

CONTENTS

BEFORE THE BEGINNING . . .

"Is this story going to be true?" my companion across the bonfire asks.

It is so dark that I can barely make out the one who said this, nor the other half dozen or more who are gathered around the fire—all of them just dark shapes, the color of granite, and still as stone.

"As true as any fairy tale," I answer.

"Well, then," he says, "true enough."

I ponder for a moment and then begin.

PART I
THE ESCAPE

CHAPTER ONE

AN OPEN DOOR

How drowsy it all had been: the warm sun pouring through the living room window, the buzz of a fly, the ticking of the clock, the murmur of soft voices.

"The guard has fallen asleep." That was Lily.

"Shh," said Rose, the second sister.

"Take off your crinkly slip," said the third sister, Iris.

What, Tag wondered, was happening? She looked up from practicing her ABC's to see the hired guard asleep in a chair and her sisters by the door to the garden, slipping their noisy underskirts out from under their dresses.

"What are you doing?" Tag said.

"Quiet!" Rose whispered.

Three sets of fingers went to three sets of lips.

"Tie your boots, Tagalong," Iris said, pointing to the little girl's feet. "Then you can come, too." She looked meaningfully at the door.

"You're going—"

"Shh!" all three hissed at their little sister.

Tag looked down at her hanging-open boots, laces trailing. She crouched to thread the laces around the hooks, a tedious process. When she finally got to the part where you loop the strings into some sort of knot and there's supposed to be a bow made by some mystery of twisty finger-magic, she was befuddled. This was the part she had always cajoled one of her sisters into doing for her.

Tag looked up, hoping to see a helpful face, but no. There was a swirl of skirts, a blur of movement, whispers, and stocking-footed tiptoeing, then a rush of fresh air as the door to the garden was opened and the skirts rushed out.

Her sisters had gone *Outside*!

There they were, out *there*, in the garden! Feeling the earth under their feet, brushing their hands along the mums, weaving asters into their hair, and skipping under a shower of copper-colored leaves with the autumn-scented air all around them. There was Lily, spinning around a slender birch, as if the tree were her dance partner. And Iris, twirling with her arms out, face tipped toward the sun. And Rose, who with a glance saw Tag running toward the open door and threw her hand up—a warning—*don't come*! (And so Tag stopped just at the threshold.)

Had Rose known? Did she know what was about to happen? Because when Tag saw that hand go up, palm first, and Rose's sweet, kind face, she hesitated. In that moment, a blast of frigid wind blew into the room as if

coming for her. As Tag cowered, the wind lifted the curtains, knocked over a lamp, and woke the guard, who leapt
up with a "What the Devil!" By the time he had left his
chair, a black cloud had swallowed the sun and snowflakes
were pouring out of the sky. The garden disappeared in
an angry whirl of snow, first the tops of the spruce trees,
then their trunks, then suddenly, everything was hidden
behind a thick, white veil.

Almost as fast as the storm had appeared, it dissipated.
The dark clouds receded, the garden reappeared, the snow
melted. Everything was just as it had always been, except
Tag's sisters were gone.

CHAPTER TWO

AN UNEXPECTED
MESSAGE

Seven years later, the house had become quiet and dark. Every window boarded over. Every door but one turned into walls. And only the ticking of the clock and the creak of the floorboards to disturb the stillness.

What Tag now knew of Outside is what she could see from a round knothole in the wooden plank that covered the place where the French doors once were. If you make a circle with your thumb and middle finger, you will see how much of Outside Tag could see.

The knothole was big enough to press an eye against, or poke her nose out of, or even her tongue to get a taste of falling snow. A snow-flake, she discovered, melts even before it touches your tongue,

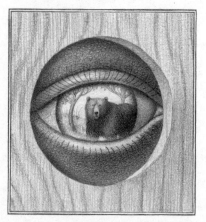

with a taste as clear as sunlight. A taste Tag imagined was like faraway kingdoms that she was told did not exist.

Still, Tag knew some things that were there, outside that circle. There were three big pine trees out of eyeshot. She knew they were there—she could smell them for one thing. And the wind in their crowns sang their shapes: soprano, alto, tenor—tall, taller, tallest. There was a stream she'd never seen, but it described its shape, chattering over the stones in its way, murmuring as it slowed and circled in a deep pool. Tag could see it all in her mind's eye.

As far as she could tell, Outside was all movement and sound: the ground alive with hopping birds chirping their delight when their efforts turned up a bug or worm. Ducks waddled up from the stream, shaking themselves dry and complaining about everything. Flocks of juncos startled and took flight, their white tail feathers flashing. She sometimes thought she'd like to take wing with them.

From her knothole, Tag could see the trail the deer had made through the yard. And the paths of rabbits leading under the hedge and those of squirrels worn into the bark of the big white pine. Even the birds seemed to follow invisible paths in the sky. Where did they lead, these paths? Tag wondered. Was there a path for her?

That was what she was wondering when all at once and of a sudden her view disappeared. Something had moved in front of the knothole, blocking it.

It took her a moment to realize that she was staring at another person's eye. She was about to jerk away when she remembered that this was *her* knothole to look *out of*, not a knothole for someone else to look *into*. So she stayed put.

The other eye didn't budge, either. Their eyes locked just long enough for Tag to register its color: silken gray flecked with gold. Then the other eye moved, and Tag saw the rest of the face. The face of a young person! Young like Tag.

That was one surprise. Under-fifteen-year-olds were not allowed Outside! But here one was, peeking into *her* knothole, from the Outside, looking *in*!

Another surprise came in the form of a small, rolled-up scroll of paper slipped into the knothole. Tag accepted it, pulling it all the way through.

The eye disappeared, and the face with it. Although Tag pressed her own eye to the hole, trying to see around the corner, the face was gone. But in her hand, she still clutched the scrap of paper.

Tag tiptoed to the study, where her mother was working. She pressed her ear to the door and could make out the rustle of paper. Her mother was busy and likely to stay put.

Back at the knothole, Tag carefully unrolled the little scroll of paper. It was a scrap torn from a flyer. On one side of the paper were the words *OUND OUTSIDE WILL BE PUNISHE*. The first and last letters were torn off and the words were scribbled out, although she could still read them. But on the other side of the paper—the blank side—(Tag caught her breath) was a hand-drawn invitation to a meeting that very day, with a little map showing how to get there! A map with a dotted line leading from X ("your house") to another X ("meeting place"). Tag knew what that dotted line meant. It meant a path, a path for her! And she meant to follow it. In fact, she had never wanted to do anything so much in her entire life.

But how was she ever going to get out of the house? The boarded up, locked in, caulked, sealed house that she had never left, not once in all her thirteen and a half years.

It's not as if she'd never tried! She had prowled the house over, hunting for cracks, fissures, holes that might be exploited. There was the time she tried to pry a loose board off the wall with a crowbar. Who knew that it was going to squeal like a cat with its tail caught in a meat grinder?

She tried tearing up a floorboard and managed to put a squirrel-sized hole in the floor. Squirrels had taken advantage of that.

She'd once pretended to be her own music tutor, fake mustache and all, in order to be let out of the house.

She was mulling what options were left when she heard

the click of the lock and the creaking of the kitchen door, the one door that remained.

Clutching the little scroll in her fist, Tag ran to the door, hoping it might have been left open. A moment would be all she'd need. But the door was already closed and locked by the time she reached the kitchen.

". . . the garden going to ruin," Cook was muttering as she waddled into the kitchen, carrying a kettle in one hand, a basket in the other, and a small branch under an arm. "Weeds, vines, the hedge untrimmed, the fruit trees with their branches broken by that bear."

Tag knew that bear. She'd seen it through her knothole. Once, he walked by so close, all Tag could see were the glossy bristles of his fur. But if he was far enough away, she could see his whole self, sometimes standing on his hind legs, sniffing at the apples in the tree. Wasn't it interesting that you could see something so large as a bear through such a tiny hole? Or something so small as a person's eye? Remembering, her heart gave a thump. The palm of her hand where she clutched the paper prickled.

Cook set the kettle on the stove and the basket on the kitchen table. She pushed aside the things littering the table—things she'd brought on previous trips for Tag to study: pinecones and needles of various lengths and degrees of prickliness, an assortment of leaves, pieces of bark, owl pellets, chickadee nests, blue jay and goldfinch feathers, the exoskeleton of a dragonfly (which Tag had learned was called an exuvia), the papery skin of a garter snake. Then Cook plunked the small branch in front of Tag and said, "What kind of tree is that from?"

Tag picked up one of two books on the table—*The Field Guide to Trees*—and pretended to page through it. She knew the branch was from the apple tree in the garden. She even knew which branch it was, having watched the bear break it. But the open book gave her a way to study the map. With trembling fingers, she unrolled it, pressing it flat against the page and running a finger along the dotted line, feeling as if she were already traveling it.

"It's a shame, it is," Cook was saying, clucking her tongue as she spread butter on a roll. "A shame your father squandered his fortune and sold off most of his things"—Tag didn't have to look to know that Cook was gesturing at the rest of the house, which, except for the kitchen table, was mostly bare—"trying to get your sisters back. It sent him to his grave, and now there's naught for you, poor little Hyacinth." Not even Tag's mother called her by her real name—only Cook did.

"Do you think they're out there somewhere?" Tag asked, meaning her sisters. How many times had she stared through the knothole, past the ruined garden into the distance beyond, wondering? Now she focused on the map, wondering again. "And do you think that they can still be found?"

When she looked up, Cook was gazing at the wall where there had once been a window. "I wonder," she said, then handed Tag the well-buttered roll. "Eat, my dear. You have to keep up your strength."

"Maybe if you would let me go Outside with you, I could look for them," Tag said hopefully.

"Don't you be thinking such things! You going off to rescue your sisters! Oh no. That's the kind of thing you only hear about in fairy tales."

Cook was always saying things like that, but Tag didn't even know what a fairy tale was, having never read one.

"What does that mean?" Tag asked, watching Cook slide her hand into her pocket. Was that where she kept her key?

"That's just an old saying—*that's the kind of thing you only hear about in fairy tales*," Cook said. "I don't suppose anybody remembers what it means anymore."

"But, what *are* fairy tales?"

"Oh, just made-up stories, pet. Just foolishness."

"Why aren't we youngers allowed to read them?"

This wasn't the first time Tag had asked this question, and the answers were varied. Sometimes Cook explained how years ago the Powers-That-Be—PTB for short—got rid of all the fairy-tale books, and most other books, too, because they were inappropriate, violent, and full of negative stereotypes and outdated values. Some were even dangerous! She said that books from the Other Times made people feel sad about what had been lost and bad about themselves, and nobody needed that. So now the only books anyone was allowed to own were field guides, dictionaries, and lesson books sanctioned by the PTB.

This time Cook said, "Oh, I don't know why. Nobody remembers the reasons anymore. Maybe books gave people *ideas*. Now eat!" she said, pushing another bun toward Tag.

Tag chewed on the bun while wondering where Cook kept her key. Was it in a shirt pocket, or the pocket of her cardigan? Or the pocket of the coat she was currently sliding on over these other pockets? It hardly mattered. There was not the slightest possibility that Tag could slip her fingers into any of those pockets without being noticed.

Now Cook wound her long scarf round and round her neck and waddled toward the door. Could Tag sidle out with her, she wondered, as she crept up behind her. Could she slip Outside unnoticed?

"Horrors and frights!" Cook said, spinning about and facing Tag, who was hiding behind the woman's ample self. "Have you lost your wits?" With a gentle push, she returned Tag to the kitchen while muttering, "And after what happened yesterday!" Then she disappeared through the door, giving the lock a decisive *click* behind her.

The door—solid oak and thick as a tree trunk as far as Tag could tell—stayed locked at all times. Cook had a key and Mother had a key that she kept on a chain around her neck, the key deep in the bodice of her stiff, black dress. Tag had once tried to sneak the key out from under Mama's bodice while she was sleeping. Which is when she was reminded that her mother never really slept.

Tag had already searched the entire house, hoping to find another key hidden somewhere. But she checked again, rifling through the kitchen cupboards, once filled with jars of jam and canned peaches but now nearly bare. The bread box, empty. Inside the piano, which had done little else than gather dust since the music tutor had been let go.

There was no use thinking about it, she knew already: There was no other key. So, how? How would she get Outside?

———

Tag went to her room and flung herself face down on her bed. If her sisters had been there, they would have had some ideas. They were the clever ones.

Once this house had been full of her sisters. Now they could be hard for Tag to even remember, although their scent still lingered in drawers and closets, and in the soap Tag occasionally used, when she bothered to bathe.

There was only one tangible thing Tag had from her sisters, kept inside a box that she now slid out from under her bed. One blue satin ribbon from one braid come undone.

Running it through her fingers reminded Tag of how it had been before her sisters had been windswept—the house softened with thick rugs and the sound of the piano being played, the smell of stews bubbling on the stove and cakes cooling on the table. They all wore pretty dresses then, in soft pinks or pale blues, with full skirts made fuller with crinoline slips. Each with a long braid down her back, tied with a satin ribbon.

The ribbon made her sad, too, and not just because it reminded Tag of her lost sisters but because it reminded her of herself: a flat, listless ribbon, untethered to anything. Purposeless.

But then this listless thing did something unexpected. It uncurled, like a ripple of light on the surface of the water. Almost like a living being, it slipped through her fingers, lifted up and away from her hand, coiling and uncoiling until she leapt off the bed and snatched it out of the air.

It's only my imagination, Tag whispered, stuffing it into her pocket.

The ribbon seemed to have a mind of its own, though. It rustled inside her pocket, slipped out, then floated out of the bedroom. After a startled moment, Tag rushed after it, but the ribbon eluded her, moving down the hall and up the stairs to the third floor. This was the servants' quarters, back when they had servants. But now it was empty, and Tag watched the ribbon undulate down the hall and then stop and hover in one spot.

Tag ran toward it, arm outstretched, hoping to snatch it up. But just as her hand was about to close around it, the ribbon lifted up above her head. Tag, reaching for it, noticed something she had long forgotten.

There was a door in the ceiling. Yes, there, facing downward, a door, as if the whole house had been tipped sideways. There was once a cord that dangled down from the door, she remembered . . . and now the memory rushed back in full: The tallest of her sisters, Rose, had put six-year-old Tag on her shoulders and instructed her to reach up and snag that cord and hang on for dear life. Then her sisters pulled on Tag's legs as if *she* were the cord, and the door popped open and a stairway unfolded with a clattering racket, as if by magic.

The cord was long gone now, cut by their mother when she discovered that the girls had played there. But the eye-hook that held the cord was still there, and Tag watched in wonder as the ribbon looped itself through that very hook.

All Tag had to do was to reach that ribbon and she'd be able to pull the stairs down. But she had no older sister to boost her up, nor a younger one to set on her own shoulders. So she dragged an end table into the hallway, then a stool, then a sturdy-looking box. The stool was balanced atop the table and the box atop the stool. Tag gingerly climbed on top of the teetering tower, reaching up, and a little farther up, just as the box tumbled out from under her, the stool slipped off the table, and the table toppled over with a clunk.

Clinging to the ribbon, Tag dangled like one of the crystals on the dining room chandelier. The attic door gave way with a wheeze and then, with a sudden jolt, flung itself open and ejected the clattering stairway. As the stairway came down, so did Tag. Abruptly.

There was silence while Tag listened for her mother. Had she heard the stairs clattering down? Or the tumble of the box, stool, and table? But her mother was two floors down, and since Tag heard no query from below, she must not have heard. So Tag jumped up; stuffed the ribbon into her pocket; put away the table, the stool, and the box; and bounded up the stairway.

Stepping into the attic was like emerging into another world. Unlike the rest of the house, a place emptied of its treasures, the attic was jammed floor to ceiling with boxes, bins, trunks, old suitcases, and racks of hanging clothes, everything made pale with white dust.

But Tag wasn't interested in any of this. For there, on the far wall, was a window.

CHAPTER THREE
THE ATTIC

The light coming in through that small square seemed as bright as the sun and moon combined. Not since her mother had sealed off all the windows and doors had Tag seen so much of the world at once. Nor had she ever seen the world from so high—her sisters had made her sit as a lookout at the bottom of the attic stairs, in case their mother should come looking for them.

So, this is what the world looks like, she thought, standing at the window. There's so *much* of it!

Beyond their small garden were the tops of buildings: all straight lines and hard edges, with only a few trees rising above the rooflines, each one a place to rest her eyes. Like birds, her eyes flew from one soft rounded crown to the next, until, at what must have been the far edge of the town, the landscape dissolved into the uneven undulation of forest. Beyond that were tree-lined hilltops, and beyond that, what looked like a dark crown perched on the head of the world.

She had heard whispers of mountains. Nobody talked openly about them, as if to do so would be to bring about bad luck. As she stared at them, the jagged, dark shapes seemed to shift, move, fade. They were quite clear for a moment. Then, as if a veil drifted over them, they disappeared.

Tag turned her attention to the ground below. It was very, very far away. It was a devilishly long way down.

How was she ever going to get down there? The house offered no vines of any kind, sturdy or otherwise. No handy scaffolding. No latticework. Nothing. Tag turned away from the window and surveyed the room, thinking there may be a ladder or a rope.

There were bins and boxes, and against one wall, an old wardrobe. There was a trunk full of old dress-up clothes, her father's ukulele, and a shelf on which slumped a lumpy sleeping bag and a saggy old rucksack.

On a rack of hanging winter coats, there was also a jacket of Papa's, one he'd worn when he worked in the garden. The scent of the roses and peonies he carried into the house still clung to his jacket sleeves. That was back when he was master of this house, before he was broken by grief. Tag pressed her nose to the jacket and breathed in, trying to remember those happier days.

The attic was full of her sisters. In old trunks and chests, Tag found Iris's chemistry set and microscope and her well-worn ballet slippers. Rose's books of piano music and notebooks full of math equations. Lily's canvases—painting after painting of the garden as seen through the

French doors—every brush stroke filled with longing to be *there*—Outside.

Moving aside rolls of old wallpaper and saggy cardboard boxes, Tag reached the wardrobe. When she opened the doors, it was as if her sisters rushed out—at least, the smell of them did, as if they were in there somewhere, among their trousers and party dresses, their skirts and stockings and shoes.

Tag climbed inside and sat right down among their shoes and wept. She wept until she had to wipe her face and blow her nose on the hem of a skirt. For her sisters, lost to the wind. For her father, sent to his grave. For her mother, laced into a corset of grief. And for herself, floating about the house, as untethered as the blue ribbon.

So, Tag thought, here is where her clothes had come from all these years, patiently waiting until she grew into them. Here, in this wardrobe, was her future wardrobe, at least until she outgrew her sisters.

"My name should be Tagalong Handmedown," Tag said to herself. "Queen of the Attic." A queen who needed to find a way out of her palace.

Just then, her hand bumped against a hard, square-edged thing in the far corner. Opening the door farther to let in more light, Tag saw that it was a book, an ancient-looking thing, its edges tattered and torn.

Fairy Tales from Here to There, it said on the cover, "Volume III: *Tales of the North*." An actual fairy-tale book! She

couldn't believe it. She couldn't count the number of times Mama had said, "You're not living in a fairy tale." Or Cook said, as she had that very day, "That's the kind of thing you only hear about in fairy tales."

She remembered Cook telling her once that the fact that under-fifteen-year-olds could be swept away at any time by a snow squall was enough danger for anyone. Nobody needed more danger in the form of frightening stories.

The book even *smelled* dangerous. It smelled of clouds and fiddlehead ferns, woodland campfires and castle kitchens. Or at least what Tag imagined those things might smell like.

And of course, it *was* dangerous to possess an illegal book. People were sent away—banished—for the offense.

Still, somehow, she found herself tucked into a corner of the attic with the book open on her lap. The light from the window cast a lemon-yellow circle on the book and left the rest of her in soft brown darkness. Tag read stories of golden birds, magic beanstalks, and long-haired girls locked in tall towers. She explored mountain caves and deep, dark forests and found herself hiking across a vast field with her eye on a golden castle glimmering in the far distance. She encountered witches and shape-shifters, mermaids and snow snakes, dragons and people-eating giants.

And then, in a tale titled "The Three Princesses in the Mountain Blue," she read these very words: *"The king never let his daughters out into the open before they were fifteen years old or else a snow flurry would come and take them."*

That stopped her. Tag's hand paused over the words as they sank in. "*. . . everything was so green and pretty, they just had to go out,*" she read. "*The girls pleaded with the guard to let them go, and finally he did, 'But only for a tiny, little while.' They ran all over the garden and picked armfuls of flowers and then . . . just as they leaned over to pick a beautiful rose, a big snow flurry came, and they were gone.*"

Tag set the book on her lap and took a deep breath. Here in this book was the story of her own family!

"The king had it proclaimed that the one who could rescue the princesses should get half the kingdom, his golden crown, and whichever princess he desired for a wife."

That part was strange. Tag hoped her father hadn't offered his daughters as a reward to whoever could find them!

The story went on for many more pages after this. Would the girls be rescued? If so, how? Tag had to know! But she heard footsteps—her mother in her heeled boots, which she wore even when she was napping. Her mother had been napping when her sisters were swept away; she'd had to pause to put on shoes and had never taken them off since.

Tag skimmed ahead, reading about a captain, a lieutenant, and a young soldier who set off to find the princesses. The soldier is the only one brave enough to go through both fire and water to reach, once inside a mountain, *"a large and splendid castle . . . and there sat the eldest daughter spinning copper yarn . . ."*

"Tag?" Mama's voice reached her all the way up two flights of stairs.

Tag read on. *"'I want to rescue you from the mountain,' the soldier said."*

"Tagalong!" Mama yelled, louder this time. "Where are you?"

Tag tiptoed down the attic stairs in her stocking feet. Hoping Mama wouldn't come up, she called down. "I'm on the third floor playing hide-and-seek."

"With whom?" her mother asked.

"The ghosts," Tag answered.

There was a little snort, which was the most Tag ever got out of Mama in the way of a laugh.

"I'm going out," Mama called up the stairs. "I have errands and then I'm going to the council meeting."

"All right, Mama," Tag called down the stairs. Then,

pulling out her invitation and studying it for a moment, she whispered, "I have a meeting to go to, also."

Now, she knew, was the time to get out of the house. But first, Tag returned to the book, skipping ahead to the part where the soldier finds the first princess who is being held captive inside a mountain. *"Begone!"* says the princess. *"If the troll comes home and finds you here, he'll put an end to you right away!"*

"Trolls," Tag said aloud. *"Trolls?"* The picture in the book showed a troll as a kind of almost humanlike giant, wearing almost human clothes, but with strange misshapen features, several heads with moss and ferns growing out of them, and a long, bedraggled-looking tail.

So, Mama and Cook were right about fairy tales, Tag thought. *Foolishness.*

Through the window, Tag watched her mother in her brown coat wheeling her bicycle through the garden gate. This was it! Her chance to get out. And here was a window! But she was Jack without a beanstalk. Rapunzel without long enough hair. Even if her hair *had* been long enough, Tag thought, twirling one of her braids, she could hardly climb down her own braid!

No, if she was going to climb down something, it would have to be something she made herself. After she had been caught unready—her shoelaces untied—when her sisters were windswept, she first learned how to tie her shoes. Then, thanks to *The Field Guide to Knots*, she kept learning every kind of knot there was. What if she used these old clothes to *make* a long braid? A rope of clothes—a velvet cape, some pantaloons, her mother's fur coat . . . If she twisted them like so, then knotted them together, and kept doing that—pajamas, sweaters, aprons, her sisters' party dresses . . .

As Tag twisted and knotted and tied, she tried to persuade herself that when she finished the rope, she would somehow, miraculously, be brave enough to climb down it.

At last it was done. A rope long enough to reach the ground, or thereabouts. Tag took the heavy wooden curtain rod off its hangers, tied the rope to it, and placed the rod across the window so it was fixed.

Her eye fell on the book of fairy tales. What if her mother found out she'd been in the attic and closed it off forever? She'd never get a chance to find out what happened to the windswept princesses—or what happened in all the other tales she had yet to read. She grabbed the rucksack, crammed the book of fairy tales into it, and slung the sack over her shoulders. Then she slid the window open.

The air came at her in a rush, and all the smells and scents she'd been getting in little snuffs and sniffs flowed over and around her, practically *begging* her to come Outside. She knew now there was at least one other younger out there, Outside. On the other hand, remembering what had happened to her sisters, Tag backed away from the window.

Once again, the ribbon escaped from her pocket and floated away. Light as a leaf, it was swept out the window.

Her heart went right out there with it, and next thing she knew, she'd flung the rope of clothes out the window. Following the ribbon as it drifted toward the ground, Tag climbed down the rope, hand over hand, catching the scent of anise on Lily's apron, the mothballs in her mother's coat pockets, the cedar smell of the dresses: Blue, that was Iris's, yellow was Rose's, then pink—Lily's. Tag pictured her sisters spinning and spinning, twirling their skirts so they poufed out like umbrellas. Rose and Iris would hold Tag's arms and spin her round and round until she felt like she was flying. All she saw around her was the rich gloss of fabric, the rustle of silk, a blur of blue and yellow and pink.

The memory was so strong that for a moment Tag felt as if she was reliving it. But no. What was happening was that she was falling, pulled backward by the heavy book in the rucksack. The blur of colored fabric was the rope of clothes unwinding as it tumbled down all around her. Until, at last, she thudded to earth.

Against the pale white sky, the blue ribbon drifted down and down, landing softly on her chest.

So this is how the sky looks, Tag thought: pale and vast and never-ending. And this is how the Outside smells—of pungent earth and crumpled leaves, of winter-scented air.

The air was as soft as her sisters' silk dresses and so rich and fragrant, it seemed as if you should do more than just breathe it. Taste it maybe. She'd seen that old bear stick his tongue out and lick the air—why not, she thought, giving it a try. It tasted sweet and spicy and slightly dangerous. This must be what freedom tastes like, she thought. She felt herself expanding, filling up with Outside. Soon she would be made of flickering sunlight, of crisp fresh air, of fallen leaves.

Trying to raise herself on her elbows, she found that she could not. Somehow, she was stuck to the ground. But no. It was the rucksack that was stuck, and once she had wriggled out of it, she had to yank at it until it gave way. Among a tangle of vines and undergrowth, a rake—the kind you rake dirt with, not the leaf-raking kind—lay with its tines facing up. That's what the rucksack was stuck on.

"That should get the gardener a scolding if you ask me!" Tag said. "Those tines could have punched holes clear through my back!"

What had saved her was the book of fairy tales, pierced almost all the way through by the rake tines.

The life-saving book went back into the holey ruck-sack. Then, since she couldn't very well leave an entire wardrobe's worth of clothes just lying about in the garden where they were sure to arouse suspicion, Tag crammed them into the rucksack. Dresses and trousers and scarves and pajamas and even Mama's fur coat—it seemed the rucksack had an endless amount of room. Everything fit.

Expecting the wind to come at any moment, Tag clung to the nearest tree. Then she dashed from tree to tree, clinging to each one until she realized that the wind was not coming to scoop her up. At least not yet. Not a snow-flake in sight. Just the ground under her feet. And a path to follow.

She took the map out of her back pocket, unfolded it, and followed the dotted line. Out the garden gate . . . past three big pines . . . down to the chattering stream . . . then the quiet pool, just as she had always pictured these things. She hadn't realized how full of sound the Outside would be: the urgently rushing brook, the whisper of pine boughs in the breeze, and a buzzing hum that must have been the heartbeat of the city. All of it saying, "Yes."

"Yes, this is the way," the leaves whispered.

"Keep following this path," said the gravel under her feet.

"You are going the right way," murmured the trees.

All in agreement. That this was where she should be and this was what she should be doing.

"How does she know she is on the right path?" asks one of my companions across the fire from me. His voice rumbles like distant thunder.

"How does anyone know when they are on the right path?" I ask back.

"She might be very wrong."

"She might," I agree. "Should I continue?"

"Will there be trouble?"

"There will likely be trouble."

"Then by all means," he says in his distant drumroll of a voice. "We love trouble."

CHAPTER FOUR

A LOFTY MEETING PLACE

Tag was feeling fairly confident until her eye caught a flyer posted on one of the trees:

> Youngers under the
> age of fifteen are
> not permitted in the
> Out of Doors!

And on the next tree:

> All youngers under the
> age of fifteen must stay
> inside—no exceptions!

She knew from Cook there were patrols out, hunting for youngers who were Outside. She knew that if she was caught, she would be punished. Mama would be fined. Which would not be good, because, as Tag well knew, they were broke. Then she remembered the forbidden book in her rucksack and shivered. She would just have to not get caught, that's all.

On the next tree, the flyer had been torn away—just the ragged edges remained.

The map's dotted lines and the path on which she walked ended at the trunk of an enormous tree. The tree stood next to an official-looking building that Tag was pretty sure, based on her mother's description, was the council meeting hall. While she was looking up into the tree's leafy crown, down came a ladder *thunkity-thunk* made of planks and knotted rope. This had been a day of firsts and ladders.

"Climb up!" said a voice in the leaves. A human voice.

"Look lively there!" said another.

"Don't let moss grow on you!" said someone else.

At the top, hands reached out to help her onto a platform set on the branches. There were three others there: A little old lady, a smallish monk wearing a hooded cloak, and a teeny-tiny old man with a bushy white beard who was holding a wooden spear-like thing.

They stared at Tag as if she had come from the moon.

"Where is your misguise?" said the little old man.

"Misguise?" Tag asked.

"Ren means *disguise*," said the monk. "You can't go around Outside looking like that!"

"Like what?" Tag asked.

"Like a younger," said the old lady who, strangely, was gnawing on a pinecone.

"I *am* a younger," Tag told them.

"So are we," said the others, lifting off their hats and hoods and wigs and beards to prove it.

"I'm Boots," said the monk, a lanky, dark-haired boy with either remarkably large feet or boots that were several sizes too big. He had a sparkle in his brown eyes that could have indicated friendly mischief or malice. Tag couldn't tell.

The skinny and somewhat startled-looking elderly lady said, "I'm Anton, but everyone calls me Ant." Although Ant made a respectable old lady, Tag realized he was actually a boy, a year or so younger than Tag, and that he had not just been chewing on the pinecone but consuming the thing.

"Call me Ishmael," said the tiny, white-bearded old man with white hair sticking out from under a brimmed cap, clearly younger than any of them. Too young to have even had a gender confirmation ceremony.

The monk and the old lady rolled their eyes. "That's Ren," said the monk.

"My name is Ren, R-E-N," the little younger confirmed. "I just like to introduce myself that way." Ren carried a long wooden pole with a sharpened end, held vertically, sharp point facing upward.

"Is that a spear?" Tag asked.

"No," said the eight or nine-year-old imp. "It's a harpoon."

"What's it for?"

"Usually they're used to kill whales," Ren said. "But that's not what mine is for."

"What's yours for?" Tag did not want to appear stupid, so she didn't ask what whales were.

"It's in case of pearl." Ren's eyebrows knit together in a fierce glower.

Tag looked at the others for clarification and Ant suggested, "Peril?"

"Whatever the pearl, it should fear my wrath . . ." Ren shook the harpoon menacingly, "and my lance."

Another younger climbed up from the lower branches, not in disguise either, but he looked almost old enough to get away with it. He climbed with one hand, because tucked in the other arm was a small black dog with a muzzle of bristly white whiskers and white eyebrows like furry exclamation marks.

"This is Blue Tooth," he said, setting the dog on the platform and patting its head. Within the little dog's whiskery muzzle, a black nose wiggled and twitched, constantly at work.

"Does the dog have a blue tooth?" Tag asked.

"No. It's the name of an artifact I found from the Other Times," the boy explained. With a toss of his long, black hair, he looked up at Tag and said, "I'm Finn."

Tag didn't respond. She had noticed his eyes—silken gray, flecked with gold. The eyes she'd confronted through the knothole at home.

"And you are . . . ?" he gently urged.

"Um," Tag said, still a little unsettled. "Tag. Short for Tagalong. My older sisters called me that. Because I guess I was one."

"You have sisters?"

"Had. They were windswept."

The others nodded knowingly.

"We all have siblings who were windswept," Finn said. "It's one reason we're here."

"Ah," Tag said. Then, anxious to get to the point, she asked, "What's the main reason?"

"It will all become clear," he said, gesturing to the others to follow him. "But now it's time. Let's go down."

The others climbed down a few branches, so silently that Tag didn't dare ask where they were going. She just followed along, with the rucksack still on her back. When the others positioned themselves in the branches above the courtyard outside the Meeting Hall, Tag did, too.

From the squawking and squabbling coming from below, you'd have thought there was a flock of crows filling the rows of chairs set up in the courtyard. But it was just quibbling grown-ups. From her position in the branches, Tag could see the backs of their heads. Her heart skipped a beat when she saw her mother's brown coat hanging over a chair and her hair pulled into what looked like an overbaked bun on top of her head.

The chairs faced a makeshift stage upon which about a dozen official-looking people sat behind a long table. The woman in the middle ("The council chairperson," Ren whispered, "and a beetle-headed barnacle if you ask me") banged a gavel and proclaimed, "And now for new business. Garbage pickup."

"We need to talk about the *snow squalls*! The *wind*!" someone in the crowd shouted.

"This has been going on for longer than human memory!" called out a grandmotherly woman.

"The storms are getting stronger and more frequent!" squawked someone else.

"We ask that you hold comments for the public comment period," the council chairperson said. "There are several pressing matters on the agenda we must discuss first: garbage pickup, street sweeping, market day regulations, dog licenses, and—"

"Why, after all this time, hasn't anything been *done!*" someone called out.

"Our youngers continue to be windswept," came another shout. "No one has ever been able to find them. What happens to them? Why is it so impossible to find out?"

"We want answers!" someone cried out.

"We want solutions!"

"As long as the solutions don't infringe on our freedoms!" someone else called out.

A gavel banged, the din settled into a subdued rumble, and the councilors, each with a somber voice, expressed their heartfelt sympathy and offered their thoughts and prayers to the families who had lost offspring.

"Of course, we all know it is impossible to do anything about the snow squalls themselves," the chairperson said while the other councilors chuckled and scoffed. "We can't control the forces of nature, after all!"

"In the past," continued one of the councilors, "search parties were sent out, but since no one ever returned, we had to abandon that strategy."

"Then there was the ill-conceived attempt at constructing a windscreen around the city limits," another councilor said. "As you'll recall, the wind blew it away. After that—"

"We *know!*" shouted a tall man who was standing in the back. "We know all the things that were tried. We're reminded of them every time we complain! The question is, what are you going to do *now*?"

"As to that," the chairperson said, shouting over the din, "you'll be glad to know that we will soon move into the process of serious consideration."

"So . . . you're going to . . . *think* about it?" one of the parents asked.

"Yes, we are going to think very hard," the chairperson responded.

"But is anybody going to *do* anything?"

"Yes, yes, of course, yes. We will convene to discuss the subject. And we will form a committee." The council chairperson put a finger to her temple, thinking. "Perhaps several committees. And the committees will make recommendations, and then there will be a public comment moment, and then we'll convene to take a vote, and after that, further discussion."

Some of the assembled crowd groaned and mumbled unhappily.

A person in the audience who hadn't yet spoken stood and turned to address them. "Many of you are forgetting that certain allowances must be made to keep the economy stable. And for all of you—" he swept his arm around, indicating everyone present, "to live the lifestyles to which you have become accustomed. Some sacrifice is required."

"What does that mean?" Tag whispered to Finn.

"It means a certain number of youngers have to be windswept so that olders can continue to live the way they want."

"What?" Tag said. "What did you—" Tag hushed because her mother had risen to speak.

The crowd murmured as she stood, but her mother stood silently until they settled. She was not angry or belligerent. She was calm, her voice quiet. So quiet, in fact, that listeners had to practically hold their breath to hear her.

Tag's heart was beating so hard she thought the crowd might suddenly turn and stare up at the tree, wondering where that booming sound was coming from.

"Why must it be the youngers who have to sacrifice their youth—their *childhood*, to use a forbidden word—for our selfishness," her mother said softly. "Maybe it is time for us olders to reexamine our way of life, to change the way we live and make the need for the wind unnecessary. And then perhaps the squalls would stop. Perhaps it is up to us—we olders."

The crowd sounded like a pot boiling over on the stove, hissing and spattering and bubbling. It was clear to Tag that most of the listeners didn't like her mother's idea.

As for Tag, she longed to climb down and take her mother's hand. But of course she could not reveal herself.

"Well, hmm, yes, perhaps we'll take that up in committee," the chairperson responded, "but in the meantime, certainly you should be able to control your youngers! If you want to keep them safe, it is up to you to make sure your houses are secure."

There were groans from the audience of mostly parents.

"Do you *have* youngers?" a man shouted from the back row.

"They get out! They find ways!" a woman cried.

In the tree, the youngers stifled their giggles while giving each other wide-eyed glances.

"On that point we have taken action," the chairperson said. "As of tomorrow midday, we will be adding to our regular neighborhood patrols."

"Patrols," Ren whispered, and spat. "Dog-hearted weasels."

Finn put a finger to his lips and Ren hushed.

Below them the chairperson continued. "Checkpoints will be set up at various places around town so we can apprehend any wayward youngers."

"It's just more of the same!" another parent shouted. "We want real solutions. Not more policing!"

Finn motioned to the others to climb up the branches where their voices couldn't be heard. Once they were far enough away from the crowd, he said, "I had hoped we would have more time to prepare, but what with the extra patrols and checkpoints, I think we're going to have to put our plan in motion."

"Plan?" Tag said. "What kind of plan?"

"For setting out to find our lost siblings."

"But . . ." Tag squeaked, looking around at the others. "Isn't that impossible? I mean, olders have tried. And they failed." Even though she'd been young, she still remembered how many people had gone off to look for her sisters, tempted by her father's money, and never returned. "I mean, how can we fight against wind? It's impossible!"

"Now you sound like the Powers-That-Be. The council," Ant said.

"And our parents," Ren agreed.

"But . . . *isn't* it?" Tag said. "I mean, *isn't* it impossible?"

"The council and the PTB pretend that they are trying, but they never do anything," Finn said. "Among other reasons, they have lost the ability to think in the realm of the impossible."

"The realm of the impossible," Tag repeated. "Is that a real thing?"

"It's real to us," Finn said. "And I am confident we can do it, because each of us contributes something unique and special to the effort."

Tag wondered what made her unique or special. Or if possibly she'd been mistaken for one of her sisters, all three of whom were far more talented than she.

"Now then . . ." Finn said, rolling out a map on the tree-house floor, "we enter the forest, here."

The forest on the map was indicated by circles. Yet, staring at it over Finn's shoulder, Tag could almost smell the pine needles, see the dappled sunlit path, and feel its soft dirt underfoot.

"We take this road," Finn's finger traveled along the dotted line, "through the forest into the Unknown."

"But the Unknown is . . ." Tag began.

"Unknown?" Finn finished her sentence, giving her a wink.

Again, those eyes! "Well . . . yes?" Tag managed to wiggle the words past her heart, which seemed lodged in her windpipe.

"Everything we're about to do is unknown," Finn said. "We can't be afraid of it." He turned his attention back to the map and said, "And from the Unknown to the mountains."

Tag looked down at the map, where the mountains, indicated by triangles, were colored in with dark ink. That was how they had looked from the attic window, too: rumbly jagged peaks that could just as well be storm clouds. Even the little triangles on the paper made her stomach feel tight and her heart beat a little faster.

"Are they mountains, really?" Boots asked. "My dad said they're clouds. They come and go. They're not always there."

There was a murmur of agreement, but Finn insisted, "They're mountains."

"If they are mountains, why are they only visible sometimes?" Ren asked.

"Sometimes they are obscured by fog or rain or low-hanging clouds," Finn explained. "And sometimes, I suspect, by something else."

"By *what* something else?" Tag asked.

"He means magic," Ren whispered.

"I don't know," Finn said, "but the wind that comes here has a purpose. And it doesn't come out of nowhere. It has to come from somewhere."

"And you think it comes out of the mountains," Boots said. "Where you think our siblings are."

Tag caught her breath. She remembered that in the fairy tale about the girls who were blown away in a snow flurry, all three of them were found inside mountains. At the very end of the story, the princess tells her father, *"Here's the man who rescued us from the trolls in the mountain."*

It seemed unlikely that their siblings were held captive by trolls, like they were in fairy tales, but then who would ever believe there was a place where children were threatened by meteorological conditions? Or that there would be a place on earth where their parents, their elders, and their government would do so little to keep them safe?

CHAPTER FIVE

THEY START OUT

N o more time," Finn said, shouldering his rucksack. "The meeting will adjourn soon, and we have to get going before it does." He lowered the ladder and started down.

The others started to follow, but Ren said, "Wait." And, turning to Tag, commanded, "You need a misguise. You can't go out there looking like that."

"Is she coming along?" Boots whispered.

"You know I can hear you, right?" Tag said.

The others stared at her for a moment and then resumed whispering while Tag dug around in her rucksack for a disguise. While she pulled out her mother's fur coat, she caught snatches of their conversation (*"She doesn't seem to know anything." "I don't think she's been out much."*) Or at *all*, Tag almost added, putting the coat on over the rucksack, which gave her a satisfyingly stooped-over appearance.

"Finn invited her, so there must be a reason," whispered Ren, as Tag draped a shawl over her head and tied it under her chin.

"Are you youngers coming along or are you going to stand around here clucking like chickens?" Tag asked them in a scratchy voice, peeping out from under the shawl.

"You look like a small bear in a babushka," said Boots. He had a way of pressing his lips into a tight little knot as if to keep himself from giggling—or maybe to keep from saying something smart-alecky.

"I aspire to be a bear," she told him.

"You aspire *me* to want to be a bear," Ren said, starting down the ladder.

Tag wasn't entirely sure what Ren meant by that but didn't ask, just followed after the other two. Boots stayed to pull the ladder up, then descended the tree, swinging from branch to branch and finally crashing to earth, leaves and twigs showering all around him.

Once they were all gathered at the base of the tree and Boots had dusted himself off, Finn began to explain what would happen next. Tag heard him telling them where to go from there, how to avoid being seen, and where to meet, but she wasn't paying attention. It was dawning on her that this was really happening, that she was about to leave home, not just for an afternoon but for nobody knew how long. She was thinking about the buns that Cook left on the table, and the soup on the stove . . . and of her mother—how would her mother fare when the last of her offspring disappeared?

". . . at the big, yellow three if we get separated. Got it?" Finn was saying when Tag tuned back in.

The others nodded, and since everyone else did, so did Tag. They all fell in line behind Finn, following him down narrow alleyways and quiet streets. Branches, leaves, and twigs that littered the streets from the previous night's squall crunched underfoot. The houses and buildings they passed were quiet—many of them as empty as the snail shells or shed snakeskins that Cook brought for Tag to study.

But trees and plants sprouted from every little patch of dirt, and Tag kept falling behind because she wanted to feel the oak's wrinkled bark or run her hand along the beech tree's smooth skin.

So this is what tree bark feels like, Tag would think. Or this is what the ground under your feet feels like, or so this is a mud puddle, she might think, having just stepped in one. So this is what it feels like to have friends.

Or was it? Tag wasn't sure. It's not like she belonged to the group, because she didn't. She'd never belonged to her sisters' group, either. She'd always just been the tagalong, and she guessed she still was.

Her companions hurried along, sticking to the shadows or trying to stay close to walls. But it didn't take long to see they needn't have been so careful. None of the olders who were Outside paid them any mind! The youngers caught glimpses of workers in white coveralls shoveling leaves into wheelbarrows. Groups of olders—people in raggedy coats and others well-dressed who looked like they had more important things to be attending to—were busily picking something up off the ground, tucking what they found into bags or sacks or even their pockets.

"What are they doing?" Tag whispered to Ren, who was just ahead of her.

Ren scooped a leaf off the ground and handed it to Tag.

It was a leaf unlike any other Tag had ever seen or felt—leathery, and a little heavier than an ordinary leaf.

"You have to—" Ren reached up and rubbed away the dust that coated the leaf, revealing a silvery gleam.

"Why are people collecting these? What is it?" Tag asked.

"That's currently," Ren explained.

"*Currency*, Ren means," Ant said. "In other words, money. And really, the only people authorized to pick those up are the PTB footlickers in the white jumpsuits. But everybody goes out anyway, and they're all so busy trying to get as much as they can that nobody pays much attention to anyone else."

"But . . . why do people want them?" Tag asked.

"They use them to pay for things," Ant explained. "They're valuable."

"Why?"

"Why what?"

"Why are they valuable?"

"I don't know. They just are!"

"I suppose it's really just because everyone agrees that they are," Ren said. "It wouldn't work otherwise. Everyone has to agree that each leaf has a certain value so you can use them to pay for things you need or want."

"Like food," Ant said.

"And clothes, houses, things like that," Ren finished. "The more leaves you have, the more things you can buy."

"Don't your parents go out and collect them after a snow squall?" Ant asked.

Tag shook her head.

"How do they buy things?" Ren asked, but didn't wait for an answer, scooting off with Ant to catch up to Finn and Boots.

How *had* her mother been buying things? Tag wondered, pausing to admire the bright shimmer of a few errant snowflakes dancing in the air—leftovers from the previous day's snow squall, she supposed. Leaves—red, gold, yellow, burgundy—drifted down from the trees, trees she saw for the first time in all their immensity, bottom to top. That's when she noticed that none of the trees had leaves like the silver one in her hand.

She ran to catch up with the others. "Where do these leaves come from?" she asked.

"Not from any trees around here," Finn said. "They blow in with the wind. That's the only time you find them."

The others hurried on, but Tag stopped for a moment, staring at the leaf in her hand. She was about to press for more information when the back of her neck prickled, and she glanced over her shoulder, expecting to see someone.

But there was nothing. No one was there.

She stopped again to stare up into that leafy kingdom, then felt a hand tugging at her sleeve.

"Step lively, there!" Ren hissed at her. "We don't want the scurvy devils to notice us."

"Who?"

"The patrols," Ant said.

"I don't see any patrols." Tag glanced about while stumbling along after them.

"Of course you don't!" said Ren. "They're invincible."

"What?" Tag asked. "They're what?"

"Invisible," Ant said.

"I mean invisible," Ren confirmed. "But they're not *litterly* invisible."

"They wear chameleon suits," Ant explained, "that are made of fabric that changes to look like the surroundings. It's almost impossible to see them—they wear hoods and masks and gloves and everything, so unless they pull their hood off or something, you can't see them."

"But *they* can see *you*!" Ren chirped. "And they are villainous dogs, so let's go!"

Ren and Ant jogged to catch up to Boots while Tag paused to look around her. She saw no one. And yet branches moved as if pushed aside. Leaves scattered as if someone moved through them. There was the crack of a twig. The crunch of leaves.

Tag picked up the hem of her coat and fled, racing after Ren. Is this what life in the Outside is like, she wondered? Full of beauty, but also fear? Could you have just one or the other? Or must they always go hand in hand?

CHAPTER SIX
THE RUINS

On a hill, Tag watched Finn gesture to the others to "get down," and they all flopped on their bellies and started to wiggle-crawl toward the top. Crouching, Tag hurried to catch up, then creep-crawled up the hill until she reached the summit.

There they looked down on what must have been miles of old, falling down buildings. The roofs had mostly collapsed, and what had been doors and windows were now just gaping holes. Whatever had been inside had long since rotted or been carted away. Unused, the walls of the structures had softened to rounded lumps and were grown over with moss and vines. Big, open areas stretched out in every direction, the ancient, cracked pavement sprouting with weeds and trees. Broken glass, bits of trash, and tattered strips of plastic poked up from the dirt as if trying to grow into something more impressive. Warning, danger, and "no trespassing" signs were on every tree, post, or stump.

DANGER!
STAY OUT!

"The Ruins," Finn whispered reverently. His eyes swept over the ruined buildings. "I'm just scanning the area for patrols."

"Me too," said Boots as he shimmied up a nearby tree.

"How would you know if they're here?" Tag asked. "I mean, since they're invisible."

"You have to look for something that isn't quite right," Finn said quietly. "When they move, there's a strange waver. Sometimes they're careless. Sometimes they leave footprints."

"Hey!" Boots called out from his perch in the tree. He held a hand over his eyes, scanning the distance. "I see it! I see the Big Yellow Three!"

They all looked up, and in the far distance Tag could just make out a tall, almost monumental, shape. From the ground you couldn't see the whole thing, but you could tell it was once yellow, maybe bright yellow. Now it was kind of a pale mustard color, splotched with red rust.

"Let's head for it." Finn squinted down on the Ruins as he added, "It seems safe, but we should move swiftly through here. You can ditch your disguises now."

Boots dropped—or maybe fell—out of the tree, and they all struggled out of cassocks and dresses, flinging aside wigs, hats, and suspenders. Tag tried to get her coat off, but it kept getting hung up on the rucksack.

As the others were slipping out of their disguises, Finn said, "Once we get to the Big Yellow Three, we're at the end of the Ruins, and not long after we'll come to the Unknown."

Tag gave up wrestling with her coat and asked, "Have you been there?"

"If I had, I'd call it something else. 'The Known,' maybe." Finn gave her a wink. Then, noticing the others were back in their regular clothes, he said, "We can go. But be careful. There could still be patrols."

Boots ran down the hill into the Ruins, scrambled up a wall, and danced along its crumbling edge. They watched as he came to a gap in the wall and leapt to the next section—or tried to. He didn't quite make it. Off he went again, climbing and jumping and slipping and stumbling.

Ren turned to Finn and asked, "Aren't you going to stop him?"

"Why?" Finn said.

"*Why?*" Ren said, with hands on hips. "He's making spectacles of himself. And what if he fractures his clavichord or sprains his uncle?"

Finn shrugged, saying, "He seems sort of indestructible."

"What if the wind comes and he's out there all by himself?" Ren cried.

"Well, you have a point there," Finn conceded. He shouted at Boots to come back.

Boots turned, waved, lost his balance, and toppled to the ground.

Muttering curses, Ren added for Tag's benefit, "Is he even worth saving from himself?"

NO TRESPASSING!
THIS AREA IS
PATROLLED.

The rest of the group hurried along what had once been a roadway but now was little more than a foot trail, with weeds and plants struggling to grow through the cracked and pitted pavement.

"Tansy, knotweed, buckthorn . . ." Tag murmured the plants' names as she passed, touching their stems and leaves, delighted to see in real life the things she'd memorized from her field guides.

Once again, she found herself trailing behind the others. Finn, seeing her lagging, came back to walk with her while the others marched on, their eyes trained on the Big Yellow Three in the distance.

"What *was* this place?" Tag asked as Finn approached.

"Nobody knows for sure," he said, "but you can find a lot of artifacts from the Other Times here." He dug at the dirt with the toe of his shoe. "Mostly it's just bits of metal or plastic, but sometimes I find whole objects . . ." He stopped to pry something out of the ground. "Like this!" he exclaimed. Using his shirtsleeve, he rubbed the grime off the thing he'd found and handed it to Tag.

The object was made of hard plastic, with two little "wings" on each side that slid into her palms as if that was where they were meant to be.

Finn reached over and wiped more dirt off the face of it with his sleeve, revealing a bunch of buttons of different sizes, and maybe different colors, although it was hard to tell. Also, she could just barely make out the letter "X."

"What's it for?" she asked.

"I don't know! Press the buttons," he said. "Maybe something will happen."

She tried, but nothing did. "Maybe it was a musical instrument?" she wondered.

"Or maybe if you pressed the buttons in the right sequence you'd get candy slices or sugar nibs," Finn said.

"Or maybe," Tag said, getting into the spirit of it, "if you pushed this one"—she pressed down—"you could *fly*! And then you could steer yourself like this." She held the device like she'd seen her mother hold the handlebars of her bicycle, but over her head as if she were steering up to the clouds.

"That's probably it," said Finn, laughing.

"Here," she said, holding the thing out to him.

"You keep it," he said, closing her fingers around it with his own warm, rough-skinned hands.

Tag's breath caught somewhere between her chest and her throat as she felt his hands on hers.

But it was only a moment before he gestured toward the others, who had gotten far ahead of them. "We should catch up with them."

"Okay," Tag said, shoving the gift into her rucksack. "But can I ask you something?"

He turned back and she pulled the leaf from her pocket, turning it over in her hand. "So, these are valuable," she mused. "Even though they're just . . . leaves?"

"Yes," Finn said. "But they're silver. And they come only with the wind, so they're rare. I think that's why they're valuable."

"The leaves come from the wind," Tag said, as it began to dawn on her, "so olders profit when youngers disappear?"

"Yes," Finn agreed.

"So . . ." Tag went on, "it's like the wind is *paying* for the youngers it takes?"

"I don't believe it's the wind, exactly. I think the wind is controlled by something—maybe someone—else. And the council and the Powers-That-Be aren't ever going to do anything about it," Finn explained. "Some of our elders are more concerned with what would happen if the leaves stopped coming than they are about what happens to their youngers. That's why *we* have to be the ones to do something."

Is that why her once-wealthy family had become so poor, Tag wondered? Her mother was always muttering about "not profiting from tragedy." Tag had never really understood what she meant, but now she had an inkling. She'd never seen her mother with any of these leaves but remembered her leaving the house with a rolled-up rug or a lamp under an arm and returning with groceries or lesson books for Tag.

Now Tag pulled up the collar of her coat to catch the scent of her mother, then used the collar to swipe at her nose and eyes, both of which seemed to be running.

"How do you know so much about everything?" Tag asked. Why did he know so much while she knew so little?

"I live out here," he said.

"Out here? Where?"

Finn spread his arms and spun around. "All of Outside is my home."

"You don't live *in a house*?" Tag whispered.

Finn shook his head.

"But how . . . ?" Tag blinked. "I mean . . . what about the snow squalls—the wind?"

Finn gestured to his dog, who looked up at him and wagged her stubby little tail. "Blue lets me know before it comes, and I know lots of places to hide." His eyes shifted to something behind her. Before she could turn to look, he put his hand on her shoulder and whispered, "Can you run?"

She nodded.

Finn took off across the expanse of crumbled concrete, jumping over puddles and weaving around saplings and clumps of weeds. Tag tried to keep up, but the rucksack jounced against her back and the fur coat tangled between her legs, finally tripping her so thoroughly that she fell hands first into the mud.

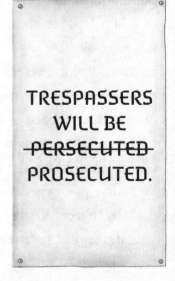

TRESPASSERS
WILL BE
~~PERSECUTED~~
PROSECUTED.

She picked herself up and was just trying to shrug off the coat when she heard a twig snap. She looked up and around, holding her breath.

"Finn?" she said quietly, knowing it was not Finn.

Gravel crunched. The sound of someone trying to step very quietly.

Tag looked and looked, trying to peer into invisibility. Trying to see people-sized shapes in the weeds and crumbled concrete walls.

Snap. Another twig.

A small stone tumbled along the ground not far away, as if someone's foot had kicked it.

A movement of air, the scent of soap, and then, with sudden swiftness, everything went black.

CHAPTER SEVEN

THE SQUALL

This is how the adventure ends, Tag thought, as something that felt like a big pillowcase was pulled over her head all the way down to her feet.

Of course, she struggled and flailed, lashing out, kicking and punching, but it was hard to land a punch when she couldn't see what she was punching at! She felt herself being flung over someone's shoulder, jouncing and jostling as she was carried along.

She remembered the same unpleasant sensation from when her sisters rolled her up in a sheet and tickled her. They were merciless! The only way to make them stop was to play dead. Go completely limp. Eventually they would get so worried that they would unwrap her to make sure she wasn't dead. That's when she would leap up like a wild cat, hissing and clawing, startling her sisters long enough to make a break for it.

What would happen if she tried that same tactic now? In a kind of paroxysm, Tag stiffened her body, then went limp.

"That's weird," said her captor in a low rumble, like the voice of doom.

"What?" the other one, more of a squawker, asked.

"The younger. She just suddenly went limp," said the doom-voiced one. He poked her, but Tag did not and would not respond. No matter what. She doubted that anyone would be as persistent as her sisters. Or that there could be anybody more stubborn than she!

The patrols poked and prodded and jabbed and slapped, but Tag remained as limp as a possum.

"I think she's dead," said the voice of doom.

"What? No! How?" croaked the squawker. "You'll have some explaining to do if you killed a younger."

"Me?" now the doom-voiced one sounded surprisingly whiny. "I didn't do nothing. Nothing that could kill anybody, anyway!"

"Well maybe she fainted in there," said the squawker.

Tag felt herself being set down and the bag being peeled back. *Wait*, she told herself. *Wait. Wait* until the bag is all the way off.

"What's the matter with her?" said the squawker.

"Dunno," said the whiner, poking her again.

Tag did not move. Her feet were still inside the bag, and she was going to need them to make a break for it. The patrols drew very close. So close she could smell their breath, which was not good. That is, their breath was not good. It *was* good that they were so close, because with one more yank of the bag, her feet were set free.

Up she jumped, scratching and clawing, screeching like a cat. She even made contact once or twice. And the element of surprise seemed to put them off for a moment.

Blue Tooth appeared out of nowhere, barking and jumping up as if she was putting her paws on someone's legs. And wonder of wonders, little muddy pawprints appeared, as if floating in thin air.

Clots of mud came sailing through the air and splatted into the invisible figures, appearing alongside the paw prints. A human shape began to materialize.

Mud! Tag thought, lunging for a mud puddle. She scooped up two handfuls and flung them—heave-*splat*, heave-*splat*. She scooped and threw, scooped and threw. Little by little, two mud-spattered figures became visible. They were so busy trying to wipe away the muck and smearing mud all over themselves instead, they didn't think to try to grab her.

"Oh, man. We're going to be in trouble," the squawker squawked.

Suddenly Finn was there. He handed Tag the dropped rucksack, took her muddy hand in his, and pulled her along, running and running.

Ahead, she saw the others. "Patrols!" she shouted. "The patrols are coming!"

60

The others turned her direction, and then started laughing.

"Ha!" Ren laughed, pointing at the patrols. "You're not invisible anymore! You're just a couple of bespattered barnacles."

The patrols slowed, looking down at their mud-smeared bellies. Trying again to wipe off the mud, they succeeded only in slathering it onto more places. Finally, they slunk away, defeated.

The others laughed at the comical sight of the partially visible patrols sneaking away.

"If they had tails they would be tucked between their legs," Finn said.

"How did you get her away from them?" Boots asked Finn.

"You mean Tag?" Finn said. "I didn't do anything. She got away from them herself."

Boots, Ant, and Ren looked at Tag. Did she detect a hint of admiration? Or was it disbelief?

"Let's keep moving," Finn said. "We should get out of the Ruins before dark."

Tag had begun noticing small creatures darting along the edges of walls, scurrying around corners, disappearing through holes. Anxious to get out of the place, she shouldered her rucksack, draped her fur coat over her arm, and trotted along, trying to keep up with Finn. She thought about the artifact he had given her and wondered if there was anything she could give him.

The breeze had picked up. Tag could feel it on the back of her neck.

"Do we have to worry about the wind?" Tag asked, perhaps squeaking a bit. She turned back as if to take a look at it, but of course all she saw were the effects of the wind, not the wind itself: branches waving, leaves fluttering, and Finn's hair blowing all around his face.

"Keeping an eye on it," Finn said. "Or I would if my hair didn't keep getting in the way!" He laughed, tucking it behind his ears. "I should probably cut it."

"No!" she said. "Don't do that. Your hair is so . . ." She was going to say "beautiful" but was struck with shyness. But then she had a thought. She did have something she could give him! She took the ribbon from her pocket and offered it to him.

"For my hair?" he asked.

She nodded.

"Will you tie it back?" he said, turning his back to her.

She stepped behind him and gathered his hair in her hands, then looped the ribbon around and around, tying his hair into a dark, glossy ponytail.

"It's kind of magic, the ribbon," she said softly, not wanting the others to hear.

"How so?" he asked without a hint of skepticism or sarcasm.

"It helped me get out of my house," she said.

"I am honored to wear it." He caught her hand and brought it to his lips, kissing it gently before letting it go.

"Ooooh oooh!" Boots and Ant sang out, "Finn and Tag, sitting in a tree, K-I-S-S—"

"You two are so immature," Ren said, cutting them off.

The more Tag tried not to blush, the more flushed her face felt. She looked toward Finn, hoping he'd say something to change the subject. But Finn was not paying attention. He was looking at Blue, whose little black nose was tipped up and twitching, a tiny, toylike growl rumbling in her chest.

Finn glanced at the sky, then yelled, "*SQUALL!*" He pointed to an age-blackened tree with a trunk as thick as a garden shed. "*TO THE BIG TREE!*" he hollered. "*RUN!*"

Ren, Boots, and Ant took off running toward the tree.

"Come on!" Finn hollered at Tag, before he and Blue Tooth dashed after the others. Already, the air was full of swirling snow and the wind was hissing through the grass.

So this is what the wind is, Tag thought, feeling it pull at her clothes and hair. *An angry monster.* It snapped and growled and gnashed its teeth. It ripped whole branches off trees, sending leaves, branches, dust, and debris spinning by. The wind sucked the breath out of your lungs and left you feeling like an empty husk with no weight or mass.

Tag paused for a moment too long. She could no longer see Finn—or anyone—through the thickly falling snow. Turning and turning, she couldn't tell which way to run.

But run she did.

As she ran, it was as if her feet barely touched the ground, and then, suddenly, they no longer did. She felt herself being lifted up, off the ground, pulled along by the wind, rising higher and higher—

And then, a hand clamped around her ankle and pulled. Just like those days when her sisters pulled on her feet to get the attic door to unfold—but this time Tag was pulled to earth.

It was Finn who had plucked her out of the air and who dragged her along toward the tree, now a dark shape looming out of the snow.

"Hang on to each other," he said as he plunked the little dog into her arms, then shoved her toward a hole in the trunk of the enormous tree. His hands gave Tag a push, but she felt them peel off her back, his palms lifting off, then his fingers—just the lightest fingertip touch before they were gone.

But other hands had hold of Tag's arms. Some hands took Blue, others pulled and yanked Tag through the hole into the tree. Once inside she saw Boots, Ant, and Ren huddled there, inside this enormous hollowed-out tree trunk. But Finn was not there.

Tag turned to look outside, but it was just a dizzying whirl of white.

CHAPTER EIGHT

THE BIG
YELLOW THREE

As suddenly as the wind had started, it ended. The tree creaked gently back into place. The silence was sudden and complete except for a kind of crunching noise. Blue, who had curled up on Tag's lap, looked up and over at Ant, who was chewing on a piece of bark.

"What do you think happened to Finn?" Boots said.

"He is probably hiding somewhere else," said Ant, with his mouth full.

"Finn must have hidey-holes all over the place, he's that smart," said Ren.

"He's too clever to get carried away by the wind," Boots agreed. "I mean, he's been living Outside for a long time."

They all nodded in agreement, but their worry permeated the air, heavy and sour. Tag hoped they were right and he was just hiding somewhere else, but she didn't think so. She was pretty sure he had been windswept and that it was her fault.

There were some furtive glances at Tag from the others. She wondered if they were thinking *she is here and our friend Finn is not. And it is because of her that he is not here.*

She desperately wanted to go home and bury her head in her pillow and cry herself to sleep. But the way back into the house—the rope—was now a bunch of jumbled garments inside her backpack. She did not think she would be able to find her way home anyway.

"He's sure to come here and get us," Ren said. "Let's just wait."

"Got any food in there?" Ant asked, pointing to Tag's rucksack.

She shook her head.

"What *is* in there?" asked Ren.

"Some old clothes," Tag said, pausing before adding, "and a book."

"Those are weird things to bring along on a quest," Boots observed.

"I didn't know I was going on a quest when I left home, did I?" Being polite, Tag didn't point out that none of the others seem to have brought *anything* along.

"What *kind* of book?" Ren asked.

Tag hesitated. It was not legal to own a book of fairy tales. There were only a few books you were allowed to possess. But then she thought, maybe the others would be a little impressed if she showed them. Maybe even forget they were angry at her. So, taking a deep breath, she pulled the book out of the rucksack and held it up, showing them the undamaged front cover.

"Fairy tales?" the others gasped. "Where'd you get that?"

"What are the stories like?" Ren asked, breathlessly.

"Are there pictures?" Ant crept closer.

"Yes, some," Tag said, opening the book. The others crowded around her, peering at the pages as she flipped through them, from one picture to the next.

"The people in the pictures are so pale!" Boots remarked. "Are they ill or something? Their skin looks almost white!"

"My granddad said that in the Other Times, people were divided up into groups by color," Ant said. "And some people were white."

"Weird," Boots mumbled.

"White people," Ren mused. "Orange people. Purple people. It sounds funny. Like calling a black-and-white dog 'Blue.'"

At the mention of her name, Blue poked her head up over the book. The dog reminded them of Finn, and they all grew quiet. Tag shut the book and shoved it back into her rucksack.

"Hey!" Boots cried suddenly. "The Big Yellow Three! That must be where Finn has gone."

***

"It's not really all that yellow, is it?" Ant mused, once they had arrived at the massive monument.

"Do you think it's really supposed to be a 'three'?" Tag wondered aloud. It hung on its post by one creaky bolt, swaying a bit when the breeze pushed it. "Maybe it used to be an 'E.'"

"Or a 'W,'" said Ren, with a tilt of the head.

"Or an 'M,'" said Ant, tipping his head the other direction.

At least at the moment, it certainly looked like a "3" and so it must be the place that Finn said to meet.

But there was no Finn.

And day was dying, the light dimming, the shadows growing longer.

Tag knew that the others were realizing what she had known all along: Their leader was not going to show up.

At last Boots said, "Well, we can't go without Finn. We have to go back."

"No!" cried Ren. "If he was windswept, don't we owe it to him to try to rescue him? Finn would try to rescue us."

"We don't have a leader," Boots said. "You're too young," he said to Ren. "Ant only thinks about food, and she"—he pointed his chin at Tag—"is nothing but trouble."

"And you are uncorrugated," Ren said.

"Uncoordinated, you mean?" Ant suggested.

"Yes," Ren confirmed. "Still, according to Finn, we each have some special talent and that's why he chose us for the quest."

Tag did not think she had any special talent, and looking around at the others, she wasn't sure about them, either. This little ragtag group likely had no business trying to rescue anybody.

Somehow Finn had made it all feel grand and possible and noble. Now when Tag looked at the others, she just saw youngers. Goofy ones. Perpetually hungry Ant, whose pants were held on with a string. Tiny but loud Ren with the gap-toothed smile, still without some second teeth. Wiry Boots, whose own boots were a few sizes too big—unless his *feet* were that big! All of them with basically no experience or knowledge of the world at large. For instance, Tag didn't even know what "the world at large" *meant*!

And yet, Tag was resolved. She was thirteen and a half years old and had not done one significant thing in her entire life. Not one single heroic thing. But that, she thought, feeling her heart swell, was about to change.

She listened while the others discussed the pros and cons of traveling without Finn. Except it was all cons. Every time Finn's name was mentioned, she felt a little more deflated, like someone stabbing little holes into her.

"Finn was the leader."

"Without Finn, we have no idea what we're doing or where we're going."

"Finn had the map."

"Finn had the plan."

"Finn knew more than all of us put together."

Stab stab stab stab stab, Tag thought. Her heart was poked full of as many holes as the pages of her book. And that made her think of the stories in that book.

She cleared her throat, and when the others turned toward her, she said, "In the stories in my book, the heroes never have maps or plans. They just set off, with stout hearts and a sense of purpose. And somehow they manage to prevail."

The others stared at her for a moment.

"The heroes are young, and . . ." she paused, trying to find a diplomatic way of putting it, and finally saying, "unlikely."

"You're saying we're unlikely heroes?" Boots said.

"Well . . ." Tag hedged.

"We are!" Ren crowed. "Look at us! We're too little, too uncoordinated, too hungry, and dumb as butterbrickle."

Tag figured she must be the "dumb as butterbrickle" one.

"How do these unlikely heroes know where they're going?" Boots asked.

"They're always meeting people—old crones or old men with long white beards who give them advice, or a magic ball of yarn, or a pair of scissors that you only have to say 'snip snip' to and it will make you a whole new set of clothes."

"Why would you need that?" Ant asked.

"The things always turn out to be just what they need for their journey," Tag answered.

"Let's say we agree to keep going," Ant said. "What will we feed the dog?"

All eyes turned to Blue Tooth, who gazed up at the youngers and gave her stubby tail a tentative wag.

"What will we feed *us*?" Ant wailed.

"Maybe Tag should go home and take the dog with her," Boots said.

Ren punched him in the arm and said, "Without Finn, maybe we need everybody we can get."

"A dog? No," Boots said. "Go home, doggie! Shoo!"

Blue tucked her tail. Her ears drooped. She gave Tag a pleading look. Tag wanted the dog along, for then she'd have at least *one* friend. "I'm sure Finn intended to take her along," she said.

"Why?"

Tag didn't really want to bring it up because it would remind everyone about how it was her fault that Finn was not with them now. But she went ahead anyway.

"It was Blue who let Finn know the snow squall was coming," she said.

The others stared down at the dog, who regarded them with chocolatey eyes and frothy white eyebrows.

"What did she do, the dog?" Boots said. "I mean to let Finn know about the squall."

Tag paused. She had just assured Blue a place with the group by making her indispensable. Could she do the same for herself? "Well, it's hard to explain, really," she said. "But I would know if I saw her do it again."

Boots's eyes somersaulted around in wild circles. "You can't just *tell* us what she did that made Finn know the squall was coming?" he whined.

Tag shook her head. "No," she said firmly. "I would have to see her do it."

"Well, then," said Ren, "that settles it. We're all in this together. And Tag is the leader."

"*What?*" all three of the others, including Tag, exclaimed.

"Why me?" Tag added.

"You have the book," Ren said. "With the instructions."

That seemed to settle it with the others, so Tag would be part of the group. And yet, she sensed that being a leader was not being part of the group so much as being *apart* from it.

Was she destined to be the outsider her whole life long? Would there ever be a time and a place where she fit in, where she felt like she truly belonged?

I get up to throw a stick of wood on the fire and one of my companions says, "You can be part of our group."

In the light of the hot flames, I can see the shaggy outline of his shoulders and his massive head. His eyes give off a dull gleam as they follow my every movement.

"All you have to do is think the way we do," he says. "And that is very easy, because we do not think very much or very hard."

"You mean, to be part of your group, I just need to see the world the way you do," I say.

"That's right."

"But what if I don't see everything just as you do?" I ask.

"Then you are thinking too much or too hard or too far out of the box. We frown upon that."

"Well, I'll think about it," I tell him.

"No!" my companions all cry at once.

"Don't think!" says one who looks as skinny as a bundle of twigs. "We don't encourage that here."

"But," says the rumbly voiced one, "do go on with your tale."

CHAPTER NINE

A COLD NIGHT

Where hat should we do first, Tag?" Ren said.

Tag looked around at the others. They were tired. It was getting dark. She wanted to say, "Let's all go home and climb into our warm beds," but she did not.

"What does your book say?" Ren asked.

Tag pretended to look for instructions in the book. "Generally," she said, "the heroes find somewhere to stop for the night."

The little group gazed sadly at the Ruins all around them, at the crumbling walls and scattered debris. It looked the opposite of inviting. Scanning the horizon, Tag saw a clump of trees that reminded her of their garden at home.

"There," she said, pointing. The others, too tired to argue, plodded off toward the grove.

As they walked, she thought perhaps now would be a good time to try to make friends. Boots was nearby, and she thought for a long time about what would be a good way to start a conversation. She chose her words carefully when she finally said, "Are your feet really that big?"

"Is your nose always so nosy?" Boots shot back.

That didn't go so well, Tag thought. She really didn't have the slightest idea of how to talk to other youngers or how to go about making friends. All she knew now was that it wasn't the way she had tried.

But after a moment Boots blurted out, "My parents got irritated by how much I like to climb on things. My mom said it 'unnerved' her. So she made me wear boots two sizes too big, to try to keep me from climbing on tables, swinging from light fixtures, and jumping down whole flights of stairs at once. Since I've got older brothers, it seems like there's always a bigger pair at the ready."

"Did it?" Tag asked. "I mean, did it slow you down?"

In answer, Boots ran up the side of a tree, grabbed hold of a branch and swung there for a while, his lips pressed together and his eyes twinkling, as if he could only just barely hold in his delight. Tag thought maybe he was trying to swing himself up onto the branch, but he lost momentum and finally gave up and dropped to the ground. Really, Tag thought, Boots's face was nearly as acrobatic as he was. His eyebrows leapt up and down, his eyes seemed to somersault in their sockets at anything requiring an eye roll. Even his ears got in on the action, wiggling and twitching as if they wanted to leap off his head and do cartwheels. But his mouth was the most agile of all, tying itself into a tight little knot as if to seal in any hilarity that might burst forth and then spreading into a wide toothy grin. In fact, his mouth flew open with the slightest provocation and out would tumble whatever thought was in his head, unabridged. And, yes, sometimes hurtful.

But this time he flashed Tag a smile that lit up the gloom. She couldn't help but smile back. Maybe she could make friends, after all, she thought, watching as Boots leapt up on a fallen tree and pranced along its trunk, finally cartwheeling off the other side. Or, well, it was something resembling a cartwheel.

Emboldened, she asked Ant how he got his name.

"It's because I can eat many times my own weight," Ant said. "Like an ant."

"I think ants can *carry* many times their own weight, not eat," Tag said.

When Ant didn't answer, she hastily added, "But they can really carry a lot. Some ants can carry fifty times their own weight—in their jaws! That'd be like us carrying a garden shed in our *teeth*!"

"I could eat a garden shed if I had enough time," Ant said.

"Wouldn't you rather eat something that's more like food?" Tag asked.

"Yes, of course," Ant replied. "But there's not always food to be had, is there?"

They both grew quiet, because neither of them wanted to talk about food that they didn't have. Even though they had been away from home for only a handful of hours, it felt like forever. The reality of their situation began to settle on Tag. Just what *would* they eat? How would they sleep? How would they stay warm during the long, cold night? These thoughts crept in along with the cool night air and the very persistent fear that would dog her every step of the way: When would the wind come for *them*?

A kind of ache settled deep in Tag's insides. So this is homesickness, she thought. Of course, she'd never felt it before, having never left home for an instant, but what else could this hollowed-out feeling be—as if some essential part of her had flown away and left just the shell behind, like the dragonfly's crusty, gray exuvia. She plunged her hands into the pockets of the fur coat, her fingers searching for the ribbon, hoping to feel its familiar satiny smoothness. But when her hands turned up empty she remembered she had used it to tie Finn's hair back, and that made her think of Finn, which made her feel very sad and frightened.

Just then, Ren's hand slipped into her own, soft as a flower petal. And she remembered she was the leader now, and so she had to be as strong as Finn.

"Night is scarier than day," Ren whispered.

"It can be," Tag agreed.

"Why *is* that?" Ant asked.

"Because it's dark and you can't see things," Boots said.

"I think it's more than that," said Ren. "There's something psycho-illogical about it."

"But we will be all right," Tag said, even though she was not at all sure about that. As shadows lengthened, all sorts of frightening things that hadn't occurred to her in the daylight began to seem possible. Even the existence of trolls did not seem so far-fetched.

When they reached the little grassy clearing surrounded by trees, Tag saw that it wasn't really like her garden, but at least it offered a feeling of safety. The straight and sturdy trunks stood around them in a protective circle, the branches knotted together overhead to create something like a roof.

Ant said he would make a fire, and after they'd gathered fallen wood, branches, and twigs, he soon had a little campfire burning.

"Good thing you brought matches," Boots said.

"And a knife!" Ren chimed in, using it to whittle bits of tinder.

"More useful than a lot of dumb clothes and a beat-up old book," Boots grumbled, casting a glance toward Tag.

"Boots!" Ren chided. "If Finn were here, he'd say we have to be respectable of one another if we are going to succeed."

"If Finn were here, we'd know what we were doing! But he isn't, and this is just a disaster. We don't know where we're going or anything. And if it weren't for her"—Boots narrowed his eyes at Tag—"Finn would still be here!"

Well, he'd said it. What everyone else was thinking. And what Tag knew was true. She had no business being there. The others maybe offered *something*. Ren, although tiny enough to disappear behind a fern, had a big voice and the courage to use it. In fact, that big voice and the way Ren hopped and flitted about reminded Tag of a bird. Boots was athletic, if somewhat "uncorrugated," as Ren said. As for Ant, well . . . he could apparently eat—and digest—anything, although she wasn't sure that qualified as a talent. But at least he'd brought along two useful things—a knife and matches—while what she had brought along was cumbersome, useless, and foolish.

Tag didn't have any special talents. Her sisters had been the talented ones in the family: the dancer, the scholar, the musician. She had always been the bothersome child who went wherever her sisters went, tried to do what they did and to be like them. But in spite of years of lessons, she still couldn't play the piano, was only a so-so student, wasn't particularly athletic, and was quite the opposite of graceful. Witness, for example, her tumble into the shrubbery from the attic window. She could not see how she had any talent at all, much less one worth taking on a quest.

"I'm so hungry!" Ant wailed.

"We're all hungry, Ant, old pal," said Boots, patting him on the shoulder.

"It's malicious-cold!" Ren shivered and rubbed those tiny hands together. "This weather is inclementine! I have goose pimples."

"Maybe I can help with that," Tag said, reaching into her rucksack and pulling out wool skirts and warm sweaters and long knitted stockings and cashmere scarves and all kinds of things that she offered to the others.

Ren chose two sweaters, wearing one like a sweater and the other like trousers, then crooned, "Cozyodious!"

"Let's hear a story from your book," Ant said, donning a large pair of wool pants and a flannel bathrobe.

By the time Tag had pulled out the book and begun paging through it, the others were bundled up in the warm clothes and snuggled close to the fire.

"What story do you want to hear?" she asked.

"How should we know?" Boots said. "We don't know any of them!"

Tag considered reading the story of the three princesses who were swept away by a snow squall but thought that might be too much like real life just now. Instead, she picked one called "Sleeping Beauty," which sounded promising, since they were all going to need to get to sleep somehow themselves.

"*In times of old there lived a king and queen,*" she began, "*and every day they said, 'Oh, if only we had a child!' Yet they never had one. Then one day, when the queen went out bathing, a frog promised her that she would have a daughter . . . and when the time came, she did! The king was so pleased, he invited many people to the christening, including twelve of the thirteen fairies of the kingdom. He had only twelve golden plates, so he had to leave one of them out.*"

Tag wasn't sure what a fairy was, but probably the others knew and, since she didn't want to seem stupid, she didn't bring it up. So she read on:

"*The fairies who were invited bestowed upon the girl many gifts: virtue, beauty, wealth, and so on, but just as the eleventh fairy was bestowing her gift, the thirteenth fairy entered the hall. Angry about not having been invited, she announced in a loud voice, 'In her fifteenth year the princess shall . . .*"

Tag stopped reading.

"Shall what?" Ren asked. "What happens next?"

"There's a hole there," Tag said.

"A hole?"

"I mean in the page." Tag showed them the punctured page.

"Are those *bullet* holes?"

"No. When I climbed out the window, I fell on a rake. Like this." She demonstrated how she fell, landing on her back. "And the book was the thing that got punctured. So now there are holes in the stories."

"Well," Ren said, "just fill them in!"

"What am I supposed to fill them in with?"

"Your *imagimination*!" Ren said.

Tag wasn't sure her *imagimination* was up to the task,

> In her fifteenth year the princess shall ☐ Without saying another word, the thirteenth fairy turned her back on everyone ☐ left the hall. Everyone was horrified, but just then the twelfth fairy stood up. She hadn't yet given a gift to the girl, and although she could not lift the evil spell, she could soften the blow. She said, "The princess shall not die but shall fall into a ☐

but she was willing to give it a try. And anyway, she was very interested in yet another girl whose precarious existence involved her fifteenth birthday.

"*In her fifteenth year, the princess shall . . .*" she said again, and paused. She didn't have any ideas.

"We'll help you fill it in," said Ren. "*In her fifteenth year, the princess shall . . .* get blown away by a snow squall!"

"On her fifteenth birthday, she would become a patrol," said Ant.

"Don't be such a realtor!" Ren said. "Anything but that!"

Tag skimmed ahead in the story and said, "Oh, no! The fairy said she would fall down dead!"

"It's always something," Boots grumbled. "You can't

even turn fifteen without either getting blown away in a snow squall or falling down dead."

"But wait!" Tag said, reading on, *"The twelfth fairy hadn't given her a gift yet, and so she softened the blow by granting the wish that 'the princess shall not die. Instead, she shall fall into a . . .'"*

"What? What will she fall into?"

"There's another hole," Tag explained, chewing on a hangnail. These holes were making it very difficult to get through the story.

"Maybe she falls into a hole in your story," Boots said, and then squeezed his lips together as if to keep himself from laughing at his own joke.

"Maybe she falls into a big pit full of rattlesnakes," said Ant.

"That's not softening the blow!" Boots said.

"Maybe she falls into a comma," said Ren.

"A coma?" Tag said. "Kind of." While the others had been conjecturing, she had read ahead. Putting two and two together, she explained to the others, "The princess doesn't die. What happens is she falls into a deep sleep that lasts for one hundred years. And not just the princess, but everybody and everything falls asleep—*"The king and queen and all their attendants, the horses in the stables, and the pigeons on the roof, the dogs in the courtyard and the flies on the wall. Yes, even the fire in the hearth flickered, died down, and slept . . ."*

Tag noticed that their own fire had turned into a sleepy

bed of coals, and her comrades were yawning and curling up under their heaps of clothes, resting their heads on their arms. She gave the coals a poke, and flames roused as if waking, casting enough light for her to read on. *". . . and the roasting meat stopped spitting and the cook let go the kitchen boy whose hair she was going to pull, and the maid let fall the fowl she was plucking and fell asleep."*

"Even Ant fell asleep!" Ren exclaimed, laughing.

Sure enough, Ant's eyes were closed in sleep while gentle snores escaped his wide-open mouth.

Boots tossed a log on the fire as Tag went on to finish the story. *"As the kingdom slumbered,"* she read, *"around the castle there sprang up a hedge of thorns, higher and higher, so that you couldn't see any of it anymore.*

"From time to time, princes came and tried to break through the hedge and get to the castle, but anybody who tried to get through got caught up in them and died a miserable death.

"On the day the hundred years had ended, the very day on which the princess was to wake up, another prince came by. When the prince approached the hedge, he found nothing but beautiful flowers lining a pathway to the castle. In the courtyard, he saw the king and queen and horses and the spotted hunting dogs lying asleep and the cat and everything else that was still asleep.

"Finally, he came to the tower, climbed the stairs, and opened the door to find the sleeping princess. Her beauty was so marvelous that he

couldn't resist kissing her. As his lips touched hers, the princess opened her eyes, woke up, and looked at him fondly."

"Wha-at?" Boots said.

"Then the king and queen woke up along with the entire court. The horses in the courtyard stood up and shook themselves. The hunting dogs jumped around and wagged their tails. The pigeons on the roof lifted their heads and flew off into the fields. The fire in the kitchen flared up, flickered, and cooked the meat. The cook gave the kitchen boy such a box on the ear that he let out a cry, while the maid finished plucking the chicken."

"That is one powerful kiss, to wake up all those things," said Boots.

"So the girl has to lie there waiting for one hundred years for the right fellow to kiss her?" Ren said. "He shouldn't go around kissing sleeping girls. He should ask first."

"I think the kiss was coincidence," Tag said. "It says right in the story that the hundred years were up; she was going to wake up anyway."

"What's the point of having a prince then? He just goes around thinking it was the work of his lips, all this waking up?" Boots complained. "Pfft."

"This story is like us in reverse," Ren said. "The princess slept for one hundred years *after* she turned fifteen. We sleep for one hundred years *until* we are fifteen."

Neither Tag nor Boots could dispute what Ren said, for it certainly *felt* true.

Ant hoisted himself up to ask, "How does it end?"

Tag quickly finished the story, reading, "*And the wedding of the prince with the sleeping beauty was celebrated in great splendor and they lived happily to the end of their days.*"

"I guess they must have liked each other then, the prince and the princess," Ren mumbled from under piles of sweaters and shawls.

Tag looked up from the book at the others, now layered under silk and brocade, velvet, flannel, and cashmere, with the fire warming them (at least on one side) and their faces glowing in its light. She draped her mother's fur coat over her and plumped up her pillow of party dresses. Blue snuggled into the crook of her knees, a warm little heater. By the time Tag closed her eyes, she was glad she had lugged along the book of fairy tales. Thanks to the story, for a little while and when they needed it most, they had forgotten their troubles. And they were left with the hope and the feeling that, like in the story, everything would turn out all right.

PART II
THE JOURNEY

CHAPTER TEN

INTO THE UNKNOWN

The next morning, Tag awoke to a crunching sound that turned out to be Ant gnawing on a chunk of bark. "I'm so hungry I could eat this whole tree!" he said with his mouth full.

"What does your book say to do now?" Ren asked Tag.

Without even looking at the book, Tag said, "Find food."

Everyone thought that was a reasonable idea. But when they emerged from their little grove of trees, all they saw were grassy fields with a few crumbling walls peeking up above the weeds and the distant, charcoal-colored outline of their town, now so far away as to seem almost imaginary. The road they were following wound through the fields and disappeared into a dark smudge in the distance. Beyond the dark line rose the jagged edges of what surely must be the mountains.

"What is that?" Ren asked, reaching for Tag's hand.

"The mountains?" Tag said.

"No, *that*," Ren said, pointing at the place where the road disappeared into the darkness.

"That must be the Unknown," Tag said. Her heart seemed to run ahead of her toward that dark place, racing with both anticipation and fear. "And that"—she paused to take a deep breath and square her shoulders—"is where we have to go."

<hr>

The road wound through tall, copper-colored grasses. Rusted metal skeletons of ancient machines rose above the weeds, and here and there long metal strips, like the ribs of large animals, protruded out of the dirt, with shreds of plastic clinging to them like pieces of hide.

When the youngers finally arrived at the smudgy dark line, it turned out to be a forest. Tag had read a little bit about forests in *The Field Guide to Trees*, but nothing had prepared her for the feeling of being in one.

"So this is a forest," she said softly. Not a few trees or even a grove of trees such as they had slept in, but a real forest that stretched on and on in every direction, a whole extended family of trees and plants—ancient grandparents, young ones, even babies.

She stood for a moment in their shadowy coolness, looking up toward the light that crept in through the cracks in the canopy, speckling the ground, leaves, and her upturned face.

For a while as they walked deeper into the wood, Tag forgot her hunger, filling up with the delicious layer cake of smells: sun-warmed pine, fallen leaves, damp earth, moldering things. She gulped in big citrusy drafts of lime-colored air while sunshine seeped into her pores. Everything about the day settled inside her like sweetened meringue.

Still, as the day went on, her stomach reminded her that although the rest of her may have felt full, *it* remained quite empty. Maybe, she thought, a story could distract them from their hunger the way it had distracted them from their fear the night before.

But she could remember only bits and pieces of the stories, so as they walked, Tag told little snippets of the tales: About bears leaving porridge to cool and a golden-haired girl who came and ate it all. About a little girl in a red cloak who carried a basket of cakes and a little pot of butter to her sick grandmother. And about a fish who swallowed a ring, and then, when the fish was cooked and served—"Well, um, there was a hole in the page there," she explained.

"Can't you tell any that aren't about *food*?" Ant mumbled around the stalk of grass in his mouth. "You're making me even hungrier."

"It's all I can think of," Tag admitted.

"It's all any of us can think about!" Boots cried.

"Shh!" Ren hushed them. "Listen."

They stopped, and they all heard it: wind. Maybe not the hungry, howling wind of the day before, but noise in the trees and the rattling of ferns and brush along the road. Near town, Finn had known about the hollow tree. But out here in field and forest, if the wind were to come for them, *really* come for them, what would they do? If the wind wanted them, it could surely pluck them out of wherever they were and sweep them away.

The travelers walked along without speaking, taking careful, quiet steps. Perhaps, Tag reasoned, if the wind could not hear them, it could not come for them.

So now there was only the soft thud of their footsteps on the trail, the occasional swish of fabric or crunch of a twig underfoot, and the sound of the wind in the trees: a whoosh, then a lull, then another stronger whoosh. Each whoosh reminding them: *I can come for you anytime . . .*

(pause)

Anytime.

In and out of the trees they went, quietly like this, sometimes coming out into a grassy meadow where they could see the far-off mountains, or what might be mountains, although they could just as well have been storm clouds.

And then they found themselves in a grove of slender trees with gleaming white bark, each one glowing as if with an inner light, like a tall, bright spirit. You could not help but be happy among them, Tag thought. She turned to look for Finn to say something about that, but of course then she remembered. It had been like that with her sisters, too, after they were windswept—always thinking of things she wanted to tell or ask them, then the ache of remembering that they were gone.

Among these trees there was a little sign that read:

> **First Sister Goat Farm**
> **Goat products,**
> **Advice given,**
> **Directions offered,**
> **Occasional spells cast**

Beyond the sign lay a small cottage with grass growing on the roof and a curl of smoke coming out of the chimney. Ant raced ahead of them, reaching the house before the others.

"This house looks good enough to eat," he said, breaking off a small piece of siding and chewing on it.

"That is disgustipating," said Ren.

An old woman came to the door. It was hard not to stare at her white hair, which looked as if it had been tied into knots.

The others pushed Tag forward and she managed to squeak out, "Please, ma'am, we're going to the mountains to rescue our siblings and we haven't anything to eat."

"We are very hungry!" Ant chimed in. "You wouldn't have anything to spare?"

"You know how to milk a goat?" the old woman asked.

They all shook their heads. How would they have ever had occasion to milk a goat?

"Well, you'll figure it out," she said. "Just a moment." The old woman hobbled into the cottage, then returned with her arms full of containers.

"One for each of you," she said, passing them out. "To put the milk in."

But now the youngers saw that what she had given them were not containers at all, but sieves. Strainers!

The youngers stared down through the wire mesh at the ground below.

"How are we supposed to put milk in this?" Boots asked, looking through the strainer at the old woman. "It'll run right through!"

"Most things worth doing are at least a little bit difficult," she answered. "Bring milk back in those and you will be well rewarded. But not a drop must be spilled *and*," she added, looking pointedly at Ant, "not a drop must be *sipped*."

The youngers nodded, more out of politeness than comprehension, as the old woman shuffled back inside the house and closed the door behind her.

At first there was grumbling: *It's impossible! You can't carry milk in a sieve! Let's just go somewhere else.* And then they just stared glumly at the goats, which were grazing on grassy hillsides or among the trees. One was tearing at tufts of grass on top of the cottage's sod roof.

In the quiet, Tag became aware of a gentle tapping sound, almost like someone impatiently rapping a pencil on a table. It was as if the breeze was trying to get their attention by rattling the loose edges of the papery bark of the trees.

"Birch bark!" Tag said suddenly, remembering what she'd read about birch trees in *The Field Guide to Trees.* "The bark is waterproof."

"This?" Ant said, starting to peel away a strip of white bark from a tree.

"Don't peel it from living trees," Tag yelped. "That can kill them!"

"So . . ." Ant said, "if this bark is waterproof, we could make a container for goat milk with it?"

"Maybe?" Tag said. "We could take the bark from fallen trees and logs."

"But the lady said we had to bring the milk back in these!" Ren said, holding up the sieve.

"What if we make a kind of liner out of birch bark, and put that *inside* the sieve?" Boots said. "Then we would still be carrying the milk the way she asked."

There were plenty of dead trees and logs about, and the youngers soon had their arms filled with bark, smooth and rosy on one side, powdery white on the other. With this, they fashioned inserts for their sieves, with the smooth side forming the inside of the container, and the rougher, papery side resting against the metal mesh.

Then it was just a matter of catching the goats.

"We should work together to catch and milk them," Ren said.

Nobody paid Ren any mind. Boots wanted the brown and white one. Ant claimed the one with the black ear. Tag chose a smallish all-white one.

Off they each dashed, chasing after their chosen goat. Blue got into the spirit, barking and yipping at first this one, then another. The goats scooted away, or twisted out of their grasp, and after a goodly time *not* catching goats, Boots stood on the roof of the shed howling with frustration, and the others sat on the ground, slumped against the shed walls.

"I am exacerbated!" Ren cried out, exasperated. "What did I already say? I already said that we need to work together! Why must I be the voice of reason?"

They started again, this time working together to catch the goats. And, working together, they milked each goat until, at last, all the birch bark-lined sieves were filled.

Ant lifted his container to his lips, and Tag said, "Stop! Don't you remember what the goat lady said?"

"One little sip can't hurt," Ant said, and took a large gulp. "I'm like to perish from hunger."

"In the stories," Tag warned, "when the characters do something they're told not to—"

But Ant had the container tipped back and his mouth open, guzzling away.

The others stared as Ant drained the container of milk, smacked his lips, and let out a satisfied sigh.

"You have a big milk mustache now," Ren said.

"And that's not all!" Tag said.

"Look at your head!" Boots cried.

Boots, Ren, and Tag stared in wonder at something very, very strange that was happening on the top of Ant's head.

CHAPTER ELEVEN

THE FIRST SISTER DISPENSES ADVICE AND AN UNUSUAL GIFT

How am I supposed to look at my own head?" Ant said, eyeing the others, who were staring at it.

The others watched as, before their eyes, small, nubbin-like bumps emerged, then grew into bony protuberances that continued to grow longer and stranger, finally splitting into several narrowing points.

"Ant!" Ren cried, eyes like saucers. "You've grown Ant-lers!"

Ant reached up and gingerly touched the horns growing out of his head, running his fingers along the complicated tangle, then tugging at them. "They don't come off!" he said in a horrified whisper.

"What do we do now?" Boots said.

"What's dung is dung," Ren said. "We'd better take the rest of the milk back to the house."

"Maybe the farm woman can help," Tag offered hopefully.

Careful not to spill a drop, they carried the other containers back to the cottage and offered them to the woman.

"Where's the fourth?" she asked. Then she caught sight of Ant. "Hmm."

"Is there anything you can do for him? I mean, can you fix, um, *that*?" Ren asked, pointing at the antlers growing out of Ant's head.

"He didn't mean any harm," Tag added. "We're all a little rough at the edges, on account of living indoors all our lives and not meeting very many people."

"Don't worry," the farm woman said. "They'll fall off eventually. But you take care now because most spells are much harder to remove or reverse. And the closer you get to the mountains, the worse and more permanent such enchantments are likely to be."

"Can you tell us how to get there?" Tag asked. "To the mountains?"

"Oh, as to that," the old woman said. *"You'll get there too late or never at all."*

"But if that's where the windswepts have gone, that's where we have to go!" Tag cried.

The old woman shook her head. "If you're bound to try, you're going to need something in your bellies. Come in." She swung the door open to reveal her kitchen table covered with golden loaves of bread, still warm and steaming from the oven. The fragrance wafted out to them, making Tag almost weak in the knees.

"Call me Vestri," the woman said, and invited them to sit at the table. She disappeared into the recesses of her cottage carrying the three containers of milk. Soon after, she returned with a big tray of small cheeses—rounds and cylinders and squares. Some white as snow, some a dark cream color, and some a nutty brown.

"What did you say you're looking for in the mountains?" Vestri asked, while wrapping a wheel of cheese in crinkly white paper.

"Our saplings," Ren said.

"*Siblings*, that is," Tag explained. "They were windswept."

"Which wind was it that swept them away? East, west, north, or south?" Vestri asked as she continued to wrap each of the cheeses in paper.

The youngers looked at each other. Nobody knew.

"Finn would have known," Boots grumbled.

Ren gave him a little kick in the shin.

"Is it important?" Tag asked.

"Would I have brought it up if it wasn't?" Vestri said.

"Possibly," Boots muttered, rubbing his shin.

The old woman shot Boots a look that could have soured milk. Having finished wrapping all the cheeses, she began cutting thick slices of brown bread.

Tag, watching hungrily, asked, "How could we find out which wind it was?"

"You'll just have to ask them," Vestri said.

"Ask who?"

"The winds!"

"How . . . ?" Tag said. "I mean, how do we go about asking the wind?"

Boots twirled his finger around his ear, indicating *crazy*, and Ren elbowed him.

"If you want to know anything about the winds, you have to ask the birds," said Vestri. "They know what the winds are up to."

Boots now twirled both fingers around both ears until Ren hissed at him to stop.

But Tag hadn't given up. "And how would we go about asking the birds?"

"Well, you could always have a chat with the trees," said the woman. "Trees know quite a bit about birds."

Everything paused for a moment as the old woman spread creamy white butter on the slices of bread and passed them around. The youngers bit into the warm bread, and for a while, the only sound was chewing and little smacks of pleasure and unplanned coos and hums and "yums."

"But tell me," said Vestri, "what makes you think your siblings are in the mountains?"

"Well, we don't really know, to be honest," Tag said. "All we have to go on is a friend's hunch and a story in a fairy-tale book. So, not what you'd call solid evidence."

"Let me see this book," said Vestri, reaching toward Tag with wiggling fingers.

Tag licked the butter off her own fingers, pulled the book out of her bag, and gave it to the older woman.

Examining it, Vestri said, "Oh, I see. These aren't stories *written* by fairies. These are stories that have fairies—or some kind of magic—*in* them. But I bet it was fairies that punched these holes here." She poked a long finger into one of the holes.

"Actually, it was a rake," Tag said.

"Lying with its tines up?"

"Yes, that's right."

"That's fairies' doing, all right," said Vestri. "That's *just* the sort of thing they'll do, the little buggers." She worked at loosening one of the knots in her hair. "Well, if you're going all that way, you'd best take this cheese with you." She filled their arms and stuffed their pockets with the paper-wrapped chunks of cheese.

"And you can't very well be eating the cheese without bread, can you?" she added. "So, take this bread, too. Here." She lifted the corners of the tablecloth and tied them around the bread so that it made a bundle and was about to hand it to Ant when she thought better of it and gave it to Boots instead. "Now, here's what you should remember. When the bread and cheese is gone and you find yourself hungry again, you should lay that cloth out and say, 'Cloth, spread thyself,' and the cloth will supply you with all good things to eat."

"Cloth, spread thyself," Ant muttered. "I'll remember."

"Yes, I daresay you will." The woman chuckled.

"*Thyself?*" Boots said, a little disbelieving.

"It's an old-fashioned tablecloth," the woman said. "Vintage, you might say."

As she showed them to the door, she gave them a warning. "You be watching out for fairies now. They can be mean little rascals. Think nothin' of poking you in the eye with a sharp stick or tying your hair in knots while you sleep," she said, while untangling another of the knots in her own hair.

The youngers unconsciously touched their hair, perhaps thinking of the fairies they'd read about in the story the previous night. Those fairies had enough magic power to put a fifteen-year-old to sleep for one hundred years! A little hair-tying would be nothing for them.

"Now, if you're going to the mountains, you'd best start watching out for trolls," the woman said.

"Trolls?" Tag asked in a whisper, remembering the trolls she'd recently encountered in her fairy-tale reading.

"Trolls?" the others asked. "What are trolls?"

"You needn't worry about them during the daylight hours," Vestri said, starting to close the door. "Only at night."

"But we do need to worry about them at night?" Ren squeaked.

"Oh, my, yes."

"But . . ." Tag said, before the farmwoman disappeared. "As to the mountains . . . how do we *get* there?"

"Keep the sun on your right shoulder in the morning and on your left shoulder in the afternoon."

"And then we'll get to the mountains?"

"No, then you'll get to my sister's, and she can tell you how to get to the mountains." The old woman closed the door, and the youngers stood outside on the doorstep.

Ant broke off a part of a shingle and took a nibble.

"Ant!" the others scolded.

"It's good! It tastes like spice cake. You should try it!" Ant held out his piece for the others.

"No!" they hollered at him. "Don't eat the nice lady's house!"

The youngers stood for a moment in the farmyard staring at the far-off mountains, now a curious shade of gray green, like something left in the fridge too long.

"Do you think there really are fairies and trolls?" Ren said cautiously. "Whatever they are?"

"Ach, no!" said Boots. "The old lady's as mad as a box of frogs."

"Somebody tied her hair in knots like that," Tag said. "Who did that?"

Boots yanked Tag's braids. "Was it fairies that tied *your* hair in knots?" he teased.

"Don't be such a beetle-head," Ren said. "Those are called *brains.*"

"*Braids,*" Tag corrected.

"I think the old lady tied her own hair in knots," Boots said. "I don't believe in fairies. I believe in hard surfaces. Here," he said, handing the tablecloth-wrapped bread to Tag. "I believe in things I can run on, spin around"—he spun himself around a slender birch, scooted up the trunk, climbing up and up, nearly to the top until his weight bent the birch's crown lower and lower—"and jump off!" he yelled as he flung himself off the tree, letting the crown lash back. As he landed, he said, "And I believe in the ground under my feet. Not fairies."

"Who did that to Ant, then?" Tag asked, shoving the bundle back at him.

"Maybe there were some serious growth hormones in that milk, or fast-working calcium," Boots said. "Fairies are just in fairy tales. Like the one you read last night. Not in real life."

"Maybe . . ." said Tag. "But I wonder . . . You know how the Powers-That-Be outlawed the reading of fairy tales? Or even possessing a book of fairy tales? Why?"

"They got rid of a lot of books because they said stories just made us feel bad about ourselves. The stories made us feel bad about how things had gone wrong, and since it wasn't *our* fault, we didn't need to read about such things."

"Okay, but why fairy tales? They're not about real things. They're, you know, make-believe. Like our cook says, 'just foolishness.'"

"I've been told that fairy tales were violent and not appropriate. Full of stereotypes. Their values are not our values anymore," said Ren.

"I heard that exact same thing!" Ant said.

"Me too," said Boots.

"What if we have all been told a *story* about why we were never allowed to read fairy tales?" Tag asked.

"You think there's a *different* reason why the Powers-That-Be don't want us reading them?" Ren asked.

"What if there's something *else* about them that's dangerous? Something about them that our elders don't want anyone to know," Tag asked.

"Like what?"

"What if they're *true*?"

I poke at the coals. When they flame up, I catch a glimpse of my companions, the edges of their bristly fur lit by the firelight, and their eyes glowing like cats'. A large, black-winged bird settles on a branch high above us and tilts its head to peer at us with one bright eye.

"What makes a true story true?" one of my companions asks.

"I guess it depends on how you define 'true,'" I tell him.

"How do you define it?"

I throw a few more sticks on the fire and glance up at that bird—a raven—to stall for time while I think about it. Truth in storytelling is a hard thing to define, because how do you explain that a made-up story can somehow also seem very, very true? And very real. Because stories—at least as far as I can tell-- are about real things like love, fear, courage, loss, and all the best and worst of human nature. But in real life there are facts, and something can only be true if it's really true.

I try to explain this to my companions, but they are unimpressed.

"Why do you make everything so hard?" the one with the serious underbite asks. "Why not just say that whatever you want to be true is true? That's what we do."

The rumbly voiced one says, "We believe what we want to believe."

"And," interjects the one who looks like nothing so much as the roots of an overturned tree, "if you can get enough people to say it's true, it becomes indisputably true."

"That is not true!" I protest. "Something is either true or it isn't, no matter how many people believe it."

A very old-looking fellow whose beard seems to be composed largely of lichen slowly rises from his spot and holds up his hand. "I'm going to say it is daytime. The sun is shining brightly."

"But it isn't," I object. "It's the middle of the night. Anybody can see that."

He turns to the others and asks, "What say you?"

"Day."

"Day."

"Day."

"Day."

"Day. Partly sunny. Light breeze. Twenty percent chance of rain."

The others turn and stare at the meteorologist among them.

"Six of us say it is daytime," says graybeard, "and only you say it is night. How can you possibly be right? You cannot. But continue on with your 'true' story."

CHAPTER TWELVE

FIRST SIGN OF TROLLS

It did not take long to run into the first sign of trolls. In fact, the first sign was a sign:

WARNING!

Beware of Trolls! Avoid being out and about between dusk and dawn. You may gain some measure of protection if you turn your clothing inside out.

"*That's* what a troll is?" Ant said, staring at the picture on the flyer.

After reading the fine print, Boots asked, "Why would turning your clothes inside out protect you?" He turned to Tag.

"How should I know?" she asked.

"You're the one with the book," Boots retorted.

"Maybe it confuses them?" Tag guessed.

"Well, I'm going to do it," Ant said, stripping off his clothes. Inevitably, his antlers got tangled in his shirt and Boots had to help get it sorted out. Then Ant put all his clothes back on, inside out.

As the youngers went on, they began to notice that the forest had grown more . . . well, just more. Everything more. The trees bigger and taller. The shadows longer, the dark darker. The duff on the ground heavier, the moss thicker. The branches overhead were so densely woven that light could barely penetrate.

"This forest must be from the Other Times, or even before, the trees are so old," Ren whispered. "It's a wonder it's still here."

Even though there were tall, old trees still standing, many had toppled sometime in the past. The long, moss-covered giants lay across the forest floor, their roots pulled out of the ground and exposed like gnarled arms or wild tendrils of hair tangled with stones and leaves.

Trolls or what might be trolls seemed to be lurking everywhere. Was that a boulder? Or the head of a troll with tufts of grassy hair and mossy eyebrows?

Even the ground they trod began to feel as if it were not ground at all but the soft, round belly of some huge sleeping being. It had slept here while the pine needles fell and piled up, while saplings sprang out of the soil that collected in the folds and creases of its skin and clothing, while the forest grew all around and on top of it.

Why else did it seem as if the very earth was breathing? From where else did this waft of air come that rimed the trees in white, if not a giant's warm breath turned to frost?

And then there was that other thing that the youngers were all trying not to think about, yet they could not think of anything else. Darkness had begun to fill in the spaces. Night—when the trolls came out—was coming on.

As the night grew darker and darker, the trail grew narrower and narrower, and finally the little group lost the trail altogether. It was so dark that they couldn't go on.

In the middle of what seemed to be the deepest, darkest part of the forest, they stopped, agreeing that they would have to camp there. Every branch and twig was so mossy and damp it was hard to get a fire started. When they finally did, it was more smoke than flame. So there they sat, trying to warm themselves in the smoke, and trying not to think about what might be lurking in the shadows or tucked behind one of these large trees.

The only one who was not downcast was Ant, who pulled from his jacket the loaf of bread and lumps of cheese. "Bon appétit!" he said, raising a round of goat cheese in one hand and a loaf of bread in the other.

Everyone else scrambled to pull their own loaves of bread and rounds of cheese from where they had tucked them in pockets or in Tag's rucksack.

For a while, there was just the sound of earnest chewing, punctuated with little sighs of contentment.

"This bread and cheese is so good it's like magic!" Ren crooned.

"It just tastes good because we are so hungry," Boots, ever the pragmatist, said.

"Magic," Ant concurred, his mouth full. Or at least that's what Tag thought he mumbled. She could only agree.

"Who wants to hear another story from Tag's book?" Ren asked.

Ant and Boots nodded and, mouths full, mumbled their assent.

Tag paged through the book, then looked up to see Ren's head swathed in a concoction of chiffon.

"What's on your head?" Ant asked. Poking at the fire, he got it to flame up so there was enough light to see.

"It's a kind of a hat," said Ren. "To keep the fairies from tying knots in my hair!"

"There is no such thing as fairies!" Boots insisted while smoothing his hair nervously.

"What about trolls? Do you believe in trolls?" Ant asked him.

"No," Boots said.

"Good," Ren said. "Let's hear a story about trolls, Tag. We better learn something about them, don't you think?"

"We're not too afraid to read a story about trolls right now?" Tag asked.

Boots shook his head. So did Ren and Ant.

Since no one dared say they were afraid, Tag began to read a story about a couple of boys who had decided to take a shortcut through the woods and "*when darkness came they lost the path, and before they knew it, they were right in the midst of the thickest part of the forest. When they realized they couldn't find their way out, they made up a fire, cut some pine branches, for they had a hatchet with them, and gathered heather and moss, of which they made a bed.*"

"You're just making this up!" said Ant.

Tag showed them the page. "Here it is in black and white. You're sure you're not too afraid to hear this story?" she asked.

"Go on," they urged. Once again, Ant stirred the fire until the flames leapt up, illuminating their faces and the pages in Tag's book.

"*After the boys had lain down,*" Tag read on, "*they heard something snuffling and snorting very hard, and they heard whatever it was tread so heavily that the earth shook under it . . . and just then they saw the trolls come rushing, and they were so big and tall that their heads were level with the tops of the fir trees.*"

Tag looked up at her quest-mates, their faces glowing from the light of the fire. She sensed something behind them, almost as if the darkness itself was gathering and taking form. Ghostly, yet dark as night, and silent.

Blue, who was at Tag's feet, lifted her head and let out an almost imperceptible growl. Did she see them too?

Three huge forms, almost human in their shape, yet with something wild and animal about them, too. And huge—beyond the scope of imagination almost. In fact, their heads were level with the tops of the trees.

"Well, go on . . ." said Ant. "What happens next?"

Tag read on, "*The trolls had only one eye among the three of them, and they took turns using it. Each had a hole in his forehead to put it in and guided it with his hands. The one who went*" *ahead had to have it, and the others went behind him and held on to him.*

"One of the boys took the hatchet and he ran around behind the three trolls and chopped the last troll's ankle so that he let out a horrible shriek. The first troll jumped in fright and dropped the eye, and the other boy wasn't slow in grabbing it up. It was bigger than two potlids put together, and it was so clear that even though the night was pitch-black, it became as light as day when he looked through it."

Tag looked up to see if she had only imagined the giants lurking in the trees. What she saw was one eye, round and white and glowing, peering down at them from behind a tangle of branches. But still she said nothing to the others and just kept reading.

"If we don't get our eye back this very minute, you'll be turned into sticks and stones!" shrieked the trolls.

"I'm not afraid of trolls or threats!" Tag called out, in the voice of the boy in the story, but as loud as she could. *"I'm afraid of neither boasting nor magic! And if you don't leave us alone, we will chop at all three of you so you will have to crawl along like creeping crawling worms!"*

When Tag glanced up again, the giantlike forms seemed to be receding, yet the eye still peered down at her. But she went on to finish the story: in return for the eye, the boys managed to finagle two buckets of gold and silver from the trolls. These they took home the next day, and *"since then, no one has ever heard that the trolls have been about in that woods again."*

Tag could barely make out the shadowy shapes, and as she watched, their eye winked shut, and the giants receded into the gloom of the forest from whence they came.

I pause in the telling of the story to stand and stretch, then poke at the bonfire.

"So," says one of my companions, "were the characters encountering trolls, or—as has happened to many other such wanderers—just the forest at night, with its shadows and strange sounds and the eerie moonlight?"

"You tell me," I say.

He laughs, a strange sound indeed—a sound of creaks and groans, of wind whistling through hollow trees. "Perhaps," he says, "it's one and the same."

CHAPTER THIRTEEN
THE TABLECLOTH

The travelers were awake and shivering at dawn. Their hair was untouched, but their socks were all mismatched, as if they had each traded a stocking with someone else in the middle of the night.

And the forest seemed transformed, making Tag wonder if they had awakened in an entirely different place. No longer dark and gloomy, their surroundings were a wonderland of shimmering moss and ferns sparkling with dew. The trees that had seemed so formidable the evening before now surrounded them like sturdy protectors. As the sun rose higher, light streamed through the treetops, warming the chilly youngers and scattering bright speckles of light on the forest floor. Tiny birds flitted among the branches, their wings silvery in the bright sun. And tiny insects, the last of the season, glittered as brightly as fairy wings.

But even amid all the beauty, it didn't take long to be reminded that their stomachs were rumbling with hunger and all the bread and cheese were gone.

"Let's try the tablecloth," Ant suggested.

"It's never going to work," Boots grumbled. "That lady was as crazy as a soup sandwich."

"It can't hurt to try," Ant said hopefully.

Boots handed over the tablecloth.

"Cloth, spread thyself," Ant said as he shook out the cloth and laid it on the ground.

They all stepped back and waited. And waited.

The tablecloth lay there, unmoving. Nor did anything appear on it.

"Like I said," Boots said.

No sooner had he spoken than a little breeze rippled the cloth. Leaves rustled overhead. A sudden puff of wind rattled the branches, and apples showered from the tree, plopping onto the tablecloth. Another little puff, and hazelnuts rained from the bushes that surrounded them, clattering onto the cloth.

The tablecloth seemed to give an audible sigh and then lay still.

"Well, that's not what I expected," Tag said, as they all stood staring at the heap of apples and nuts.

"A truly magical tablecloth would do better than this," Boots mumbled. "Like offer a platter of bacon and eggs."

"Hot toast spread with butter and orange marmalade," Ren murmured.

"Cardamom buns . . ." Tag said wistfully, thinking of the ones at home, no doubt stale by now.

"It's doing the best it can," Ant said, snatching up an apple and stuffing it into his mouth. "It's something to eat, anyway!"

"And they *are* delickable," Ren said, licking a rosy-colored apple before biting into it.

No one could disagree. The apples were as crisp and sweet as the chilly fall morning. The hazelnuts, once the youngers had figured out how to crack them, were crunchy and filling.

Tag's gaze went up into the tree. How had she not noticed that they had camped under an apple tree with hazelnut bushes all around them?

"I wonder what lunch will be," Ant mused.

———o———

In subsequent meals, the tablecloth provided plums and rose hips, nuts and seeds, wild onions and garlic. After a while, the youngers found they hardly needed the tablecloth anymore, learning how to gather their own chokecherries and crabapples, blackberries, and other wild edibles.

"How do you know about all these things?" Ren asked one day when Tag pointed out the difference between smooth-stemmed, good-to-eat purslane and hairy-stemmed, make-you-sick spurge.

"Field guides," Tag answered. "We had several." She wished she had thought to bring a couple of them along.

Instead she had brought a book of fairy tales that, although entertaining, wasn't exactly practical!

"Well, lucky we have you along or we might have already poisoned ourselves," Ren said.

Was *that* why Finn had invited her on the quest, Tag wondered?

When the little group ran out of options, they spread the tablecloth again, and it never failed to produce. They learned to enjoy the honey-flavored flowers of fireweed, tart wild cranberries, sweet mint, wood sorrel, the sharp bite of juniper berries, the anise flavor of wild fennel, and the celery-like centers of cattails.

They drank clear, cold spring water and grew hardy and strong from the fresh air, hiking, and healthy food that the tablecloth and their surroundings provided.

Later, they made sumac tea or tea from the leaves of the Labrador plant, cooked nettles, and once, near a lake, the tablecloth filled with wild rice.

"That was after they'd acquired a saucepan in which to boil water and cook the rice, and here I have gotten ahead of myself," I tell my companions.

"Yes, and you're making us hungry," says the one with a serious underbite and tusklike teeth who is eyeing me from across the fire.

This makes me uneasy, especially since he has been peeling the bark from a long branch and is now sharpening the end of it.

"And what of the wind?" says one whose voice seems to come from near her elbow. Looking closer, I see that her headscarf is simply covering a few twigs and sticks that poke out of the neck of her dress. Her head, disconnected from her torso, is tucked under her arm.

"The wind?" I choke out.

"Aye," says the head under the arm. "Tell us about the wind."

CHAPTER FOURTEEN

ABOUT THE WIND

I don't mean to make it sound like it was all sunny days and picnic lunches. It was not.

There were wasp nests, biting ants, and stinging nettles. There were ice-cold rivers to cross, hillsides of loose shale to navigate, and the occasional fairy prank to untangle, like the time the youngers woke to find all their shoelaces tied together—with knots so tight it seemed no human fingers could undo them.

Most ominously, there was the wind. Even a little gust caused the youngers to cower and flinch. A big gust sent them scrambling to hide. If no better hiding places were to be found, they would crowd into thickets, crouch behind boulders, or hide in the holes left by the roots of fallen trees.

Sometimes Tag distracted them with stories from her book about unlikely heroes doing remarkable things. Climbing beanstalks and stealing treasure. Escaping bloodthirsty witches or vanquishing dragons. But more and more, the youngers began to tell their own stories, as if the wind, unable to pull them from their hiding places, began to pull their stories from them instead.

One time, when they were tucked under a brush pile, Ren told about once having had a twin, a bigger and stronger sibling. "One afternoon, we sneaked out of the house, and the wind came for us," Ren said. "But somehow, it swept away the bigger, stronger one, and left me, the weakling, behind. I was the runk of the litter," Ren added, and nobody bothered to offer a correction.

On another day, between flashes of lightning and teeth-rattling booms of thunder, they pieced together Finn's story from what little each of them knew.

"Finn once had parents," Boots said, during a lull. "Everyone starts out with a parent or two, but Finn's parents suffered from wanderlust, that's what Finn said, and one day they just wandered away. Finn and his little brother were put in an orphanage, but we all know what happens to orphans . . ."

"What happens?" Tag asked.

A jagged, eye-piercing flash of lightning paused the conversation, leaving Tag to imagine for herself what might happen to parentless youngers when there was currency to be gained and a hungry wind to feed.

"Finn and his brother escaped the orphanage," Ant continued the story, once the thunder subsided. "They lived outside. Finn knew all the trees—the big hollow ones and the ones you could climb up into. Trees were his friends, he said, and the wind was his adversary. He and his little brother bested the wind again and again, never getting caught."

"Until once," Ren said. "When the wind got his brother."

"Actually . . ." Boots said but didn't finish. Nobody needed to be reminded of the second time, when the wind finally got Finn.

<hr />

One day, the youngers were traveling through a forest of mostly young trees—each one only as big around as one of Ren's arms—when, without warning, a bear emerged, seemingly out of nowhere. It was hard to imagine where it had been that they had not seen it until it crossed the path in front of them.

The youngers froze in place, and the bear stopped in the middle of the path and shook itself, sending a shower of dirt and leaves and grass in all directions. Then the beast turned and looked at them for a moment before stepping into the underbrush on the other side of the trail and silently disappearing.

The youngers stood riveted to the spot, not daring to breathe, unsure if they should continue on or run the other direction. And, once the bear was gone, they hardly believed they'd seen what they thought they'd seen.

Blue had been growling, although rather quietly, while keeping herself tucked behind Tag. Even after the bear was long gone, Blue kept up a little drumroll in her chest, then put a paw on Tag's leg. The girl looked down at the dog.

That's when Tag noticed—and recognized—that particular growl, the particular twitch of Blue's nose and the particular tilt to her head, as if she was listening to something far, far away, in another kingdom perhaps. Blue's eyes traveled upward, where a few lazy snowflakes drifted down from the sky.

"*SQUALL!*" Tag yelled. "Run!"

Usually, Tag kept her eye peeled for likely places to hide, but she—and the others—had been distracted by the bear and before that, Tag had to admit, she had been daydreaming about Finn.

"Where to?" the others cried. Around them the whip-thin trees waved and shook and rattled in the wind. Where could they possibly hide among a forest of saplings? And yet, the bear had seemed to pop up out of nowhere. Where had it been hiding? What had it been doing?

Tag remembered the sight of the bear shaking off dirt and forest debris. She forced herself to think. *It's fall. Bears prepare to hibernate in the fall. Bears sometimes dig themselves dens in which to hibernate, dens they line with leaves and moss and grass. Is it possible . . . ?*

"Where should we go, Tag?" Ren clung to her while the wind tugged at them both.

"Everybody hang on to each other!" Tag called, grabbing Ren's hand in hers. "And follow me!" She hoped the others were hanging on to each other, but already the snow was falling so heavily she could barely see them. Head down, she plunged into the brush where she had seen the bear emerge.

Blue scooted along ahead of them, nose to the ground. Soon, Tag knew, the snow would be coming down so thick and fast they would be unable to see anything. Already she couldn't see Blue.

"Blue!" she called.

She was answered by a high, semi-frantic yipping. Tag followed the sound to find the little dog barking at what was a well-hidden hole in the side of a hill, the opening to what could only be an animal den.

Now there was only one question: Was it *occupied?*

CHAPTER FIFTEEN

BOOTS TELLS
A STORY

The wind was swirling the falling snow into whirl-
winds around them. It was only a matter of seconds
before it would build up enough strength to sweep
them away.

"Climb in!" Tag hollered, and shoved Ren inside.
Boots wriggled in after Ren, then Ant, then Tag pushed
the whimpering Blue through the hole. Finally, Tag
dove in headfirst, but it was so crowded that she couldn't
get all the way inside.

"Is there a bear in there with you?" she said to
the others.

"Not that we've noticed," Ren said, pulling on
Tag's arms to help her in. But the wind was tugging
so hard on Tag's feet that she thought it would either
pull her out of the hole or tear her legs off. When
she finally convinced everyone to scooch in tighter
and managed to wriggle herself into the den, she

discovered that her boots had been torn from her feet, along with one stocking.

While Blue was petted and kissed and belly-rubbed by the others, Tag dug around in the rucksack, hoping that by some miracle an extra pair of shoes would turn up. But all she found was a single sock at the very bottom. Tag pondered what she was going to do without shoes while the others worried about the return of the resident bear. Those thoughts were abandoned when Boots started to tell a story.

"My parents didn't lock the doors," he said. "For sure we didn't have guards stationed at the doors—we couldn't afford that. We—my older brothers and I—could have gone out anytime, but we didn't. I don't know why. My brothers never even *looked* out. And because they didn't, I didn't. But the baby—Ori—was different. You could tell. Smarter. More curious for sure.

"So, one day, Ori was crying and carrying on and could not be soothed. All that baby wanted to do was to go Outside. It was a beautiful fall day, with leaves falling all around, and we just . . . went Outside! I set the baby on the ground and right away the sobbing turned to cooing.

"I figured that we'd go inside in a moment, but that's when I noticed the tree. We had a tree in our backyard and I'd seen it from the window, but it had never really dawned on me that a tree could be climbed. But now it did. In fact, that tree seemed to be *asking* me to climb it. Begging, really. I knew it wouldn't take me long to get up the tree, and it didn't.

"Climbing a tree was not the same as shimmying up a bannister or climbing bunkbeds. It was wondrous—the feel of the bark, its ridges that made finger and toe holds. It was like the story in Tag's book—I was Jack and the tree was my beanstalk. I was climbing into the sky! Then I got up into the branches and I could see the whole town! So many more trees to climb! So many roofs to run along, jumping from one to the next. It was as if I had come upon a kingdom as magical as any the fairy-tale Jack had found in the sky. I felt like my whole life changed right then.

"And it really did, but not the way I was imagining. Because while I was gazing out at all this wonder, I noticed a few flakes of snow. Just lazily drifting down. Then there was a sudden gust of wind so strong it ripped the leaves off the branches all around me and nearly ripped me off the tree!

"I started down, but by the time I got to the bottom, the falling snow was so thick, I couldn't see the baby.

I couldn't see anything. The wind howled. There was a blizzard of snow. I tried to make my way to Ori, but . . ."

"Why didn't the snow squall take you?" Ant wanted to know.

Boots shrugged and ducked his head.

"You didn't stay Outside, did you?" Ren said, giving him a sideways look.

Boots shook his head. "I ran inside, scared!" He sniffed and wiped his nose with the back of his hand. "I've never admitted that to anyone."

Ren patted his arm. "Who's to say any one of us wouldn't have done the same thing?"

"When my sisters were windswept," Tag said, "I paused on the threshold. I could have gone out and joined them, but I didn't. In fact, it was the only time I didn't tag along after them. I tell myself that I didn't go outside because one of my sisters held up her hand and stopped me. But that's just how I tell the story to myself. Really, I didn't follow them because I was afraid."

What Tag didn't say was that she was *still* afraid of the wind. Very afraid.

After Boots's story, they climbed out of the bear den and surveyed the damage. Tree branches, twigs, and leaves littered the ground. Grasses were flattened, as if someone had taken a big hairbrush to them. Tag's boots were hung up in the branches of the only tall tree for miles around.

Boots climbed up to retrieve them, and the others stared past him at the scudding black clouds. Behind them, the mountain peaks glowed a ghastly shade of pink.

"Does it seem to you that the mountains are changing color?" Tag asked.

The others nodded. The colors were always unpleasant, whatever they were. A dirty chartreuse, muddy orange, and now this stomach-turning shade of pink.

"We never get any closer to them," Ant said.

"Nor are they getting any closer to us," Ren said.

"We're spending too much time hiding from the wind, and that's why we're not making any progress," Boots called down from the branches. He tossed first one then the other of Tag's boots to the ground.

"I feel like we're actually getting farther away!" Tag said as she ran to retrieve them. "Is that possible? Do you think the wind has been pushing us backward?"

"At this rate, it will be winter before we get there, and I don't think any of us are prepared for that," Ren said.

The thought of the deep cold and deep snow made Tag shiver. As she pulled on her boots, she took mental inventory of the clothing left in the rucksack, which did not include winter coats or winter boots. Where would they sleep when the temperature plunged? And when the snow began to pile up, how would they continue on?

"Somehow we need to go faster or find a shorter way," she said.

"I see what looks like a signpost!" Boots called from the treetop. "That way!"

CHAPTER SIXTEEN

THE SHORTCUT TO A SHORTCUT

L ook! A double shortcut!" Ren said.

"But what is it to?" Ant asked.

"A shortcut to a shortcut to the mountains!" Boots said.

"But it points in the wrong direction if we're going

to find the other sister," Tag pointed out. "Remember how the goat lady said we should go see her sister who could tell us how to get to the mountains?"

"We don't need anyone to tell us how to get to the mountains!" Boots said. "We can see them!" Above the spire-like treetops rose the mountain peaks, just then glowing a nauseating yellowish green. "They're *right there!*" he shouted. "And that sign points straight at them."

There seemed to be no argument to that, so off they went taking the shortcut to the shortcut towards the mountains, chattering at first, then suddenly silent. That's because Blue Tooth, who was in the lead, stopped and stood stiff-legged, growling. The youngers crept up behind the little dog, peering through the blackberry bushes to see a strangely misshapen thing with a vaguely human form looming out of the surroundings.

"Is that a troll?" Ren whispered.

They stared at the strange being, with its squarish body, its tubular arms, its rusty, oddly jointed legs and blocky head. Behind it was another strange being made mostly of metal and plastic, all tied together with twine. And farther along, there was another one.

Tag thought of the trolls in her stories. "I don't think they are trolls," she said.

"I'll go check," Ren said. "You stay here."

"No, Ren!" Tag said, but it was too late. Ren was already stalking forward, with the sharp end of the harpoon pointed at the creature. A quick jab in the chest and the metal creature rocked, then settled.

"It's not even alive," Ren called back to them.

The others climbed out from behind the bushes and approached the odd being. Now they could see that the thing was made out of machines from the Other Times. Nobody knew what the machines did—none were functional anymore, at least in whatever capacity had originally been intended. But somebody had to have created these creatures. Who?

The youngers were just wondering this when they heard a sound. Blue Tooth heard it first, of course, cocking her head to one side and standing stock-still. Then the others noticed an eerie, almost wailing sound coming from farther along the path.

Tag scooped up Blue and the youngers tiptoed closer to the sound. Peeking from behind the trees, they saw a man sitting near a small campfire. He was singing and strumming a guitar. It was impossible to tell how old he was. He could be a young man who because of his hair and beard and the stooped way he played the guitar looked old, or he could be an old man whose eyes and smile still showed the young man within. In any case, Tag liked him immediately and crept closer to listen as he sang.

'Twas in the Other Times, a time of fires and flood
The towers all were toppled, the highways turned to mud
The wind, it raged, the tempests blew, the hurricane did warn
You'd better soon take shelter, shelter from the storm

Fires flared in forests, on plains, in oceans, too.
The blindness of the people caused the storms to brew
No one could imagine a place so transformed
Nowhere was there shelter, shelter from the storm

Thunder roared a warning. A wave came from the sea
Some people tried to heed it, some pretended not to see
Folks were led astray, and wrongly misinformed
While destroying their own shelter, shelter from the storm

The youngers glanced at each other, wide-eyed. Here was someone singing about the Other Times! And who seemed to know something about those times. But just as the musician was starting another verse, Blue Tooth wriggled out of Tag's arms and bounded into the clearing.

"No! Blue Tooth!" the youngers shouted, chasing after her until they burst into the clearing where a very startled human being was picking himself up off the ground. The man held one hand on his heart while using the other to dust off his pants.

"Holy hedgehogs, you startled me!" he said. He backed away, holding up a hand as if to fend them off. Was he frightened by their odd costumes? (They were all still wearing bits and pieces of Tag's escape rope.) Or perhaps by Ren's harpoon and Ant's antlers, upon which Ant had hung his jacket? Or maybe, Tag thought with a jolt, he was frightened of *them*!

"I'm sorry," the man said, almost whispering, as if someone might be listening, "but you are *youngers,* are you not?"

The youngers nodded.

"Young people such as yourselves have not been seen in these parts for . . . well, I have no idea. I've certainly never seen any hereabouts." He craned his neck, looking into the trees beyond them. "Are you *alone*? That is, are there olders with you?"

"No, we're on our own," the youngers said.

Hearing that, the musician seemed to relax. He introduced himself as Shortcut, which probably explained something, but Tag didn't bother to puzzle it out.

"But where are you bound, young travelers?" he asked.

"We are trying to get to the mountains to find our siblings, who were windswept," said Ren.

"Ooh, as to the mountains," Shortcut said. *"You'll get there too late or never at all."*

"Why do people keep saying that?" Boots cried.

"Come with me." Shortcut waved at them to follow, and they all trooped past woodpiles and piles of neatly sorted junk. Rusty, dented metal parts of one shape in one pile. Rusty, dented metal parts of a different size and shape in another. Finally, they walked through a patch of woods and up a small, rocky knob. From there, the mountains were clearly visible and pulsing with strange colors: a sort of sickening yellow, turning a stomach-churning green and back again.

"As you can see," he said, "some kind of enchantment is taking place."

"We can see that?" Ren asked. "How?"

"The colors!" he croaked. "They are a-changing. See that blue along the edges?"

Now that he mentioned it, they could see a kind of blue color oozing down from the peaks.

"I don't know what is going on in those mountains, but it can't be good," he said. "That's where the trolls live, you know."

"So you believe in trolls, too?" Boots asked.

Shortcut gave Boots a long look, then turned and started back toward the encampment. The others trotted along behind. "What I know I learned from a fragment of text—just a scrap of book page, really, but it tells of trolls who keep captives in the mountains. I suspect those captives are your 'windswepts.'"

"So the windswepts *have* been captured by trolls and they *are* in the mountains," Tag said.

"So says the text. And it goes on to say that once the mountains have turned completely blue . . ." Shortcut shook his head. "The enchantment will be complete, and it will be too late."

"Too late for what?"

"That, I don't know," he said darkly. "But trolls are involved, so it can't be good."

"Is there any way to get there in time?" Tag begged to know. "A shortcut, maybe?"

Shortcut shook his head sadly as they followed him down the path back past the woodpiles and junk piles.

"Or some way to get there faster?"

Again, Shortcut shook his head as he stopped in front of a long orange-and-black contraption on wheels. It had a row of windows along both sides and bigger ones on both ends, along with a fair number of dents and dings and rust just about everywhere. And the tires were flat.

"Allow me to introduce you to Puff," he said.

"Puff?"

"She's named after a legendary dragon from the Other Times."

"This is a *dragon*?" Ren said, whispering the word "dragon."

"This is an ISD, the seven hundred and ninth one," Shortcut said. "See?" He pointed to some faded letters on the side. "It's hard to make out, but if you look closely it says 'ISD 709.'"

"ISD stands for Inter Stellar Dragon," Ren said with so much confidence that they all just believed that it did. Even Shortcut gave a thoughtful nod.

While the outside of the ISD 709 looked the worse for wear, the inside was spiffed up something spectacular. It was outfitted with overstuffed chairs and couches set up around a woodstove, with a braided rug on the floor. Chintz curtains dressed up the windows, and little flags on a string hung from the ceiling, along with an unlikely crystal chandelier.

"This is my home!" Shortcut said proudly. "But in the Other Times, dragons like Puff were used for some very important purpose. Possibly transport. I think a driver sat here—" He plopped himself into the ripped-up seat facing the front window and put his hands on the large wheel in front of him. "And they went like blazes!"

"Did you live in those Other Times?" Ren asked.

"No," he said, chuckling. "I'm not *that* old! But I am a student of those times. In my capacity as a gatherer, I have rescued bits of music." He showed them a folder full of little scraps of sheet music.

"How do you know about those times?" Ren continued. "We heard your song."

Tag had seen sheet music for her piano lessons, but her music was sanctioned by the PTB Music Commission. These little scraps looked very old. The paper was yellowed and torn, the edges burnt and curled.

"What were they like, those times?" Ant asked.

"That's what the song was about," Shortcut explained.

"It was sad," Ren said.

"Yes," Shortcut agreed. "It is. But you didn't get to hear the last verse." He slung his guitar from his back to his front and began tuning the strings. "From the words of the immortal prophets, most of whom have been lost to time, I compiled that song," he said. "This last verse is for our times. In my own words."

Now the Earth is healing, at least it tries its best,
All of us must help it mend, let our planet rest.
We must be the healers, we must keep ourselves informed
And give each other shelter, shelter from the storm.

"What happened? How did all those things in your song come about?" Ant asked.

Shortcut shrugged and said, "The answer is blowin' in the wind, my friend."

"In the wind? The answer is in the wind?" the youngers said, startled.

"It's in one of the songs I found called 'Blowin' in the Wind.' There's a line that says, 'How many times can a man turn his head and pretend that he just doesn't see?' I think that's what happened. Humans kept turning their heads, pretending or refusing to see what they were doing to the planet. And also not doing anything about it. Or at least not enough."

"Why aren't we taught anything about those Other Times?" Ren asked.

"According to the Powers-That-Be, we'll all be happier if we don't have to understand our past. I believe what the PTB really wants is to keep us uneducated. That makes us easier to hoodwink."

"Hoodwink?" Tag asked.

"Pull a hood over our heads in order to deceive us. They don't want us to know too much. That's why they got rid of stories, you know. There are too many ideas in stories. They didn't like the songs I sang. They didn't like the questions I asked. That's why I got sent away to the borderlands. So here I am. And I wish I could help you get where you need to go, I really do, as yours is a noble quest."

"What about Puff?" Boots said. "You said dragons like Puff were used for transport."

Shortcut swung his shoulders back and smiled proudly at the orange beast.

But then his shoulders slumped, and his face fell. "Alas, it is impossible. There is no fuel to run the beast. It may have wheels, but how to propel it?"

The youngers stared glumly at the contraption; at its flat tires, its rusty self, its general rattletrappedness.

"I wonder, though . . ." Boots cast his eye at the heaps of junk and neatly stacked woodpiles. "There's plenty of wood here."

"*That* there is," Shortcut agreed.

Boots made a sketch on a piece of paper, and Shortcut seemed to catch on to whatever the younger boy was thinking. In a frenzy of movement, the two of them darted in and out of the junk piles, dragging out various scraps of metal, hinges, wire, pins, bolts, an old tank of some sort, tubing, and various bits of this and that.

Tag, Ant, and Ren sat on a pile of junk picking at stalks of grass and watching the action.

"Don't just sit there!" Shortcut yelped when he noticed them. "Start chopping wood! We'll need small pieces, not big chunks, but not as small as chips or sawdust. We're going to power old Puff with wood gasification."

Boots stood up, blew his hair out of his eyes, and grinned at the bystanders.

"How do you know how to do that?" Tag asked him.

"You're not the only one with forbidden books tucked away in the attic," Boots said. "My pop stashed away a stack of books passed down from his grandmother who had them passed down from her grandfather, and a few grandparents before that, I don't know. *Popular Mechanics*, they're called. In them I learned about something from the Other Times called an internal combustion engine."

"Yes, sir!" Shortcut's wispy hair practically stood on end with excitement. "Niños," he said, "we're gonna fly! Well, we won't literally fly. In fact, we probably won't go very fast, considering. But definitely faster than walking! Or, well, probably."

While Boots and Shortcut built the wood-burning engine and retrofitted it to the bus, Tag and Ren and Ant pumped up the tires, gave the bus a good scrubbing, made some repairs, chopped wood, and loaded it and other provisions on board.

Wood and tinder were fed into a tall steel box in the back. Thick pipes, screwed together by Shortcut, snaked along from back to front where they entered the engine.

"Are we ready?" Shortcut said when the job had been deemed finished.

"You're coming with us!" Tag exclaimed. "But will it be safe for you?"

Shortcut put a match to the wood and tinder, and smoke billowed out of the smokestack. "No, my, no!" he said. Then, as Puff roared to life, he added, "It won't be safe for any of us."

CHAPTER SEVENTEEN

ON THE WAY TO THE MOUNTAINS

After fits and stops and coughing and sputtering, they jounced and bounced over what was left of the roads from the Other Times. Who knew anything could go so fast? Surely, they would soon reach the mountains!

Out the windows, the landscape went by in a torrent of color. Falling leaves—red, gold, yellow, burgundy—flew by.

By this time, they had all forgotten the advice the goat lady had given them about finding their way to her sister's. All any of them could think about was getting to the mountains as fast as possible.

The youngers stuck their heads out the windows and hollered and sang. When the bus slowed and rolled to a stop, everyone piled out and gathered fallen branches, twigs, scraps of wood, and pinecones in the woods that lined the roadway. These they fed to the hungry engine. Then Puff leapt to life again.

Everywhere they stopped, they picked up twist ties, bottle caps, a raggedy tarp, lengths of string, bubble wrap, and plastic everything: bottles, jugs, jars, boxes, bins, lids, and bits and tinier bits. Everything they found was picked up, bagged, and stashed on board. That's because Shortcut said they should always leave wherever they were on earth in better shape than they found it.

Once they got over the excitement, they settled in. Boots slept. Ren sang. Ant spent a lot of time scratching his antlers against a table leg. And Tag read. She read the fairy-tale book as if it were a field guide, gleaning whatever information she could about what kind of enchantments trolls put on people, how enchantments were made, and how they could be broken.

In one story, a troll turned a prince into a white bear. In other stories, trolls bewitched lads into wild ducks. They regularly kidnapped princesses and carried them off to their mountain lairs. Some of these stories she read aloud, then cautioned her listeners, "You can never beat a troll with strength. They are very strong and they can use magic against you. The only way to beat them is by outwitting them."

"I don't believe in trolls," Boots said.

"You mean you think trolls are meant to be a meta-fork?" Ren asked.

"A metaphor?" Ant said.

"Yes," Ren said. "You know, they represent something. I think they represent the worst of human nature. They're motivated by greed, are only interested in power, believe untruths, are mean and mal-evil-ous. They're like some people who convince themselves that wrong is right and right is wrong."

"So you agree with me," Boots said. "There is no such thing as trolls or fairies."

"I didn't say that. I just said that *in the stories*, trolls are metaforks. I didn't say they were metaforks in real life."

⸻⸺○⸺⸻

While her companions were otherwise engaged, Tag took notes in the margins of the pages, writing down any tidbit she could learn about trolls.

- "vast, ugly, hairy giants or ogres with a malignant character" she copied from a story.
- some have multiple heads
- they may share a single eye among two or more
- they eat children
- their homes inside mountains are full of treasure that may glow at night

MARGI PREUS

Things trolls hate:
- church bells (ringing)
- thunder
- sunlight
- smell of human beings

How to protect yourself from trolls
- trick them (they are not very bright)
- turn your coat and socks inside out
- carry garlic or steel
- keep them outside until the sun rises (they turn to stone) (may also explode)

The strangest of all the troll stories was the one about the girls who were swept away by the wind. It was full of twists and turns, until at last the soldier finds the three princesses, one by one, each in a separate troll's castle inside a mountain, each sitting at a spinning wheel. One spins copper yarn, one silver, and one gold, and each one warns the soldier to go away because there is a troll, and each successive troll possesses an increasing number of heads. Each princess tells him to drink from a flask filled with a strength-giving elixir, enabling him to heft the sword that can chop off the trolls' many heads.

Tag pictured herself finding her sisters. She would swig from that flask, wipe her mouth on the back of her hand, then lift the massive sword from where it hung on the wall. She imagined her sisters looking on admiringly. She stopped short of imagining the moment when she was supposed to bring the sword down on the troll's heads as he ducked coming through the low doorway. Instead, she skipped ahead to the part where she returned home to a hero's welcome.

But if she thought about it very hard, she knew that if there were a flask filled with strength-giving elixir and a heavy sword to heft, her sisters would have already drunk from it and sliced off any offending troll heads. And escaped. But then they would have come home, and they hadn't. So Tag wondered, just what would she be required to do to rescue them when the time came? And what had prevented her sisters from doing it themselves?

At night, most of the others slept inside Puff, but Tag preferred to sleep outside under the canopy of stars or trees, depending on where they stopped. She was wary of the wind, but as long as Blue was curled up in the crook of her knees, she felt safe. Blue would wake her if a snow squall came.

Tag wished she could understand the wind. She longed to speak its language, to know what it knew, and she tried very hard to understand its voice. She listened to the way it rustled leaves on the ground or caused the uppermost boughs to nearly, *nearly* speak. It sounded so much as if they were having a conversation, the wind and the trees. The wind telling the trees where it had been, how it had billowed sheets on a distant clothesline, filled the sails of a flotilla, or blown a plastic bag across an entire continent.

Perhaps it was telling the trees what had happened to her sisters, to Finn, to all the windswepts. If she could understand the wind, then she would know if they were all right and if they could ever, ever be found.

One night, Ren crept out of the bus and climbed under the fur coat with Tag.

"Just like Queequeg," Ren said.

"Who's Queequeg?" Tag asked.

"A harpooner," Ren answered.

"Is that what you are?"

"Yes," said Ren, "but I would never harpoon a whale."

"What's a whale?" Tag asked.

"Whales were once-upon-a-time creatures," Ren explained. "The biggest mammals on earth, even though they weren't on earth, just in the sea." Ren went on to describe whales in such vivid detail that Tag had to interrupt to ask, "How do you know all this?"

"Like Ant said, you're not the only one with a forbidden book," Ren whispered conspiratorially.

Blue roused, got up, turned a few circles, and nestled back down between the two of them.

"After my twin was windswept," Ren went on, "I spent a lot of time prowling the house looking for something—anything—to help me figure out what to do. Under a loose board under a rug under a couch I found a book." Ren paused to whisper in Tag's ear: "*Moby-Dick.*"

"A book about whales?" Tag asked.

"Oh, yes. And so much more," said Ren, going on to tell the tale of the great white whale named Moby-Dick who had chomped off Captain Ahab's leg and how Ahab (who was captain of a whaling ship) had become obsessed with pursuing and killing the whale.

"When that wind swallowed up my twin," Ren said, "it was like one of my limbs had been chewed off. Now I am just like Ahab (only without the peg leg), and I want only one thing."

"To find your twin," Tag said.

"Well, *that*," Ren said. "And to get revenge."

"Revenge against the whale?"

"No. Against the wind, or whatever it is that took my twin."

They both lay back and stared up at what seemed like an ocean of stars.

Then Ren said, "In a way, I understand why the PTB got rid of so many books. Because that book made me feel both sad about what we've lost and angrish about the whale killing."

"Anguish?"

"Angrish," Ren repeated. "It's a cross between angry and anguish. But even though it made me feel that way, I'm still glad I read it. Isn't that strange?"

"Maybe I shouldn't admit this," Tag said, "but I wish we had more books. Even if they would make us feel sad or angrish."

Much later, Tag startled awake. She had been dreaming about a huge white whale moving through the ocean the way Ren had described it, its tail crashing down with great slaps against the water, and every spout issuing forth with a putrid smell like seaweed, dead fish, rotten eggs, and lack of proper dental care. It was a smell so foul it woke her from her dream.

When she opened her eyes, it was dark enough that she couldn't see anything but the yellow moon, but she had the sense of something very large standing over her. Then she saw that what she had thought was the moon was a single glowing eyeball. When the actual moon slid out from behind a cloud, she caught a glimpse of the face that eyeball belonged to, along with a mouthful of teeth as jagged as saw blades.

The face drew nearer. The disgusting breath washed over her. The teeth glinted fiercely in the moonlight.

Tag tried to scream, but her throat was tied in a knot. No sound came out.

With a sudden eruption from the covers, Blue Tooth leapt up and with a wild howling cry launched herself at the monster, sinking her teeth into the giant's nose.

Roaring in pain, surprise, or anger, the monster staggered back a few steps, clutching at the dog, still with her teeth embedded in its nose. In the darkness, Tag could just make out Blue Tooth's white muzzle and white eyebrows.

"You carrion rogue!" Tag heard Ren hollering, the spear point of the harpoon flashing, "I'll mince you up for the try-pots!"

The giant lumbered off, the dog still dangling from its nose. Then Blue dropped off, but instead of running back, she kept after the beast, barking and barking.

In the darkness, Tag could see very little, but she heard the cracking and breaking of trees and the whoosh as they fell, the crash as they hit the ground, and the thunderous thud of the giant's footfall.

The others skittered down the steps of the ISD 709 as Ren shouted, "A horrible giant monster came here! Blue is chasing it away!"

Shortcut fired up the ISD and switched on the head-lights, illuminating the backside of a shaggy beast with a humanlike form disappearing through the thick forest.

"Puff can't get through there," Shortcut said. "You'll have to follow on foot. I'll head that direction on the road as best I can and hope to intercept the giant that way."

Blue's high, plaintive yowl propelled the youngers to follow. They made their way through the dense forest, climbing over the toppled trees, avoiding broken branches, and pushing through briar and bramble. Finally, they stumbled out into a wide plain, scattered with boulders and clumps of heather, everything lit a pale gray by the moon.

The hulking shape of what was surely a troll rose out of the mist. Then, as the youngers watched, the giant turned and, with one paw-like hand, plucked up the wildly barking dog by the scruff of the neck and lumbered away into the distance.

The sound of Blue's distressed yipping drifted back to them, and Tag could just make out her bristly white muzzle sticking out from under the giant's arm. As they watched, although the eyes of the youngers never left the troll, the barking stopped, and both troll and captive sud-denly and strangely seemed to shimmer away, until they were no more.

The fire is dying and one of my companions kicks the unburned end of a log into the flames. Sparks fly up into the darkness like angry wasps. The raven flaps its wings, lifts up, and moves to a branch away from the sparks.

"You know the thing you've been calling 'Puff' is a bus," says the one who seems to be composed mostly of sticks interwoven with small stones, twist ties, and dried grass.

"A bus, huh?" I acknowledge, tucking that piece of information away.

"In Other Times, there were lots of buses, filled twice a day with plump, juicy schoolchildren."

"Youngers?" I ask.

"Aye. In Other Times, 'youngers' were called 'children.'"

"Oh, yes," says the voice under the arm. "We used to sit on that hill over there"—her free arm gestures to a dark mound in the distance— "and drool at the thought of all that tender goodness."

"Am I supposed to believe that you were around in the Other Times?" I ask.

"You forget how old we are," says the old graybeard.

"How old are you?" I ask.

"Old enough to remember when people used to ring church bells to scare us away," says the twigs and sticks one while nibbling at his tail.

"As for me," says graybeard, "that hill those others remember sitting on? I remember when it was a mountain."

"We remember those Other Times, and even the times before then," rumbles the one with a voice like thunder. "Terrible things happened during those times."

My companions nod their many heads.

"Also wonderful things."

They nod again.

"The terrible things were humans!" one of the younger ones calls out. "And the wonderful things were trolls!"

"Har." They laugh with their giant maws open wide so that I expect great clouds of bats to swoop out.

"Humans are incomprehensible," one of them says when they get over their laughing fit. "They are capable of both the best and the worst behavior, but they can't seem to make up their minds which it will be."

"There are times when we can hardly tell ourselves apart, trolls and humans," says the one with four heads. "Humans have shown themselves capable of behavior as bad as our own."

"Unlike humans, we have embraced our badness," says one head.

"We revel in it," says another.

"We excel at it," says one more.

"You sound like you're trying to talk yourselves into it," I tell him. "Maybe you're not really as bad as you think you are."

"No. We are."

"For instance," says one of those heads, "we're planning to roast you as soon as the coals are ready or your story is over, whichever comes first. Is that bad enough for you?"

"I had hoped you'd given up on that idea," I say.

There is a lot of chuckling over this. Or what I think is chuckling. It sounds more like a crowd of badgers tearing up rotten logs.

"But, by all means, go on with your tale!" Graybeard encourages me by prodding me with a sharpened stick.

CHAPTER EIGHTEEN

CATCHING THE WIND IN A NET

How did they disappear like that?" Ant wondered. "One moment we could see the monster loping across the meadow, and the next it was like they evaporated into thin air."

"I should have let the miscreant have it!" Ren said, shaking the harpoon.

"We have to get Blue back!" Tag cried. Something pinged in her chest, like one of Shortcut's guitar strings breaking loose.

As the youngers circled the spot, round and round, snow began to fall, thick and fast, like pillowcases full of it were being torn open and dumped out of the sky.

"How will we ever find Shortcut in all this snow?" Ant wondered, shaking the fluffy stuff from his antlers.

"How will we ever find Blue?"

"What if the wind comes? How will we find anywhere to hide? I can't see a thing!"

"What should we do, Tag?" Ren asked.

"I don't know!" Tag wailed. Everything seemed so hopeless. Snow piled up on her head, coated her shoulders, weighed her eyelashes down. She plunged her hands into her pockets and felt the artifact from Finn. If she pressed the buttons, could she conjure him back? But, no. She knew she'd have to find a way out of the dilemma herself.

"Look for a sign," she said.

"What kind of a sign?" Ant said.

"Any kind!" Tag squawked, waving her arm. Her hand, still holding the gizmo from Finn, knocked a clump of snow off a branch. Except it wasn't a branch. It was a signpost. And tacked to it was a sign.

SECOND SISTER, bringer of dawn
wind CONSULTATIONS and
compass readings
MISCELLANEOUS SPELLS AND
BEWITCHMENTS
advice and directions offered

Out of the snow appeared an old woman wearing a long, full skirt and carrying a glowing lantern. A floppy hat covered her hair and shaded a nose so long that Boots said she could use it to roast marshmallows.

"Are you the second sister?" Tag asked as the woman hobbled toward them.

"I take it you've met my first sister," the woman said, eyeing Ant's antlers. "I'm the second. My name is Austri." She swept the snow off her nose and suddenly the snow stopped falling and a current of warm air rushed around them, almost as if the woman had conjured it. Then she swung the lantern to and fro, and it seemed to cast so much light that even the sky itself brightened and the snow on the ground turned a rosy pink.

"What is your errand here?" Austri asked them.

"Our little dog was carried away by a, by a . . . well, I guess it was a troll! And we have to get her back!" Tag blurted out. "Do you know where they might have gone?"

"No, but soon the West Wind will come along and he should know, for he puffs and blows both hither and yon. I can ask him."

"You're going to ask the wind?" Boots said.

"Yes, but you'll have to catch him first. I've gotten too stiff in the joints to do that sort of thing anymore. Here, you can use this." Austri pulled out what looked like a butterfly net from under her voluminous skirt and handed it to Boots.

"You want me to catch the wind in a *net*?" he said incredulously.

"No? Not a net? How about this then?" This time Austri

produced a saucepan from within the folds of her skirt, along with its lid. These she handed to Tag.

Tag eyed both skeptically. "I don't see how . . ." she began.

"Not a saucepan either?" the woman said with a sigh. "Fine." She plunged her hands into the pockets of her skirt and pulled out a couple of mugs, handing these to Ant. "How about those?"

"It's impossible to catch the wind in a net, pots, pans, mugs—or anything!" Boots said. "Everybody knows that."

"Young people today give up so easily," she muttered. "One would think you'd be willing to at least *try*."

"Maybe she could snag the wind with that nose," Boots mumbled.

Austri turned her glittering eyes on Boots. "You should be careful," she said, "lest instead of words, *worms* start falling from your mouth."

"*I'll* try to catch the wind!" Ren piped up. "What can *I* use?"

The woman began to hunt in her pockets, first one and then the other until she produced a shiny gold thimble.

"Surely one of you can catch the wind in one of these wind catchers," Austri said, handing the thimble to Ren. "You're not helpless, after all! Here comes the West Wind now."

The wind came rushing in with a roar, swooping up the

fallen snow and sending it spiraling in the air. It whooshed around in big circles and billowed the old woman's skirt. It tugged at the youngers' clothes and pulled at their hair, and they clung to each other while looking around for a safe place to hide.

"Don't worry!" said the woman. "This is just an ordinary wind. It won't sweep you away."

As if offended by that comment, the wind blew the hat off Austri's head.

"No offense meant!" Austri shouted into the wind, and the gust settled. "Well?" she said to the youngers. "The wind isn't going to catch itself!"

So off they dashed, leaping and spinning, swooping or scooping or swinging their containers, trying to capture the puffs and gusts and blasts of wind. Soon even Boots was swinging his net through the air, just in case the wind *was* catchable.

Maybe it was silly what they were doing, Tag thought as she scooped with her saucepan, but at least she wasn't cowering from the wind. And, anyway, maybe it wasn't completely *impossible* to catch the wind. She'd read a story about a boy who went to find the north wind that had blown away all the flour he'd been carrying. He had a fruitful conversation with the wind and ended up richer by far because of it. In another story, a girl conversed with all four of the winds, finally catching a ride with the north

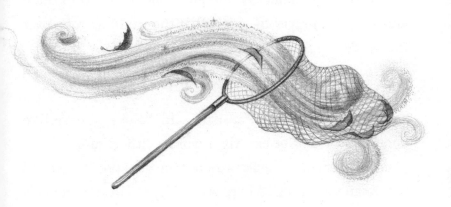

wind to a castle that lay east of the sun and west of the moon. Maybe the stories *were* just foolishness, like Cook said. But maybe, just maybe, they were not.

The night returned to stillness. The wind had either continued on its way or maybe they had caught it after all. The youngers' arms drooped with fatigue, but they clung to their containers as Austri tottered over to them and peeked into each one, lifting the lid of the saucepan and pressing an eye to Ant's mugs.

"Ah, there you are!" she said finally, peeking into Ren's thimble. "Now, Wind," she said into the tiny vessel. "Can you tell us where the troll and the little dog have gone?"

Austri waited, her ear tipped as if listening. The youngers were quiet, too (except Boots, who groaned), but no matter how hard they listened, they couldn't hear anything.

After a few moments, the old woman turned to them and said, "I'm sorry to report that the troll has gone over the border."

"Border? What border?" Tag asked. "Did they cross into another country?"

"Not a country, no," Austri said. "No, it's more like another world. Not exactly a world, either, more like a plane of existence. A place where time does not correspond to human reckoning. Where very little, in fact, corresponds to human reckoning. In this other plane, the vibratory rate is different than in this plane. Those in that world can materialize in our world at will, or, as you recently witnessed, *de*materialize, but it's not so easy for regular people. The main way humans can get through or over or past or—what's the preposition I'm looking for?—*beyond*, I guess you would say, is to be invited in, or for some reason allowed in, or as is the case with your dog—*taken* in."

Tag remembered the way the troll and Blue had seemed to shimmer for a moment and then were just . . . gone!

"It sounds difficult," Ant said.

"Indeed," said Austri. "It is impossible. But then, so was catching the wind, was it not?" She winked.

"Will crossing the border take us very far out of our way?" Tag asked. "Ultimately, we have to get to the mountains."

"As to the mountains," Austri said, "you'll get there too late or never at all."

"Why does everyone keep saying that?" Boots howled, throwing his arms in the air.

"But if you're bound to try," Austri went on, "keep the sun on your right shoulder in the morning and your left shoulder in the afternoon."

"And that will take us to the mountains?"

"No, that will take you to Nordri, our third sister. You must go there first if you ever hope to get to the mountains. She may be able to undo that spell that has befallen your friend," she went on, eyeing Ant's elaborate antlers, then turning a pale eye on Boots. "And any other spells or mishaps that may occur."

Boots could not keep his eyes from rolling around and around like marbles in a bowl.

"Thank you for the advice," Tag said. "Here is your cookpot." She held out the saucepan to Austri.

"Oh, you can keep those things," Austri said. "Who knows? They may come in handy. Now, in crossing the border, you must remember two very important things," she continued. "The first thing is, the more footsteps you take, the more you leave behind."

"Oh, mercy," Boots mumbled.

"The second thing is," Austri went on, seeming not to have heard him, "the sun rises in the east, sets in the west, and it takes but one day." The old woman started to toddle away.

"That lady is completely crackers!" Boots blurted out.

"Ick! Boots!" Ant said, his voice shaking with horror. "Things are falling from your mouth!"

"You think I don't know that?" Boots choked out, spitting a few bugs and beetles onto the ground, and also a toad, which hopped away into the underbrush. He bent over, spitting, then wiped his mouth with his sleeve.

Tag ran after the woman. "Oh, please!" she cried. "Can you take the spell back?"

Austri turned to look at the girl, the light in her green eyes like shadows flickering among ferns.

"Boots has a good heart," Tag went on. "It's just that he feels responsible for one of his siblings—a baby—and it makes him sad."

"Sad?"

"Well, the sadness comes out as grumpiness," Tag admitted.

"I only know how to cast the spells. I don't know how to undo them," said the sorceress. "But I *will* tell you how you might get over the border. At the four hinges of the day—dawn, noon, twilight, and midnight—a wee hole may open between this world and the one you want to enter."

Glancing at the brightening sky, Tag said, "We'll try for the soonest time. Dawn." Strangely, the lighter the sky became, the more the old woman seemed to fade away.

Austri put her papery hand on Tag's cheek and said, "I hope that boy knows how lucky he is to have a friend like you."

"Can I ask you one more thing?" Tag called to the rapidly disappearing woman. "Did we—did Ren—really catch the wind?"

"Sometimes," the old woman said, dissolving into the pale predawn light, "it's important just to try."

"You know what I like in a friend?" my companion across the fire says.

I get up to poke at the coals and catch a glimpse of his face. A serious underbite means that some long, tusklike teeth protrude over his upper lip. His face is as furry as the rest of him, and his forehead looms, shelflike, over his three, small, calculating, yellow eyes.

"My idea of a good friend is someone who will lie for me, maybe even steal for me. Someone who will hold a grudge on my behalf or who is jealous of others on my behalf. Someone who says bad things about others behind their backs to make me feel better."

"Someone like that," I interject, "is likely to do the same to you. Anybody who says bad things about others behind their backs is probably saying bad things about you behind your back."

"How would you know? Do you even have any friends?"

"Yes, I do," I tell him.

The raven chooses that moment to let out a raucous croak, and we all look up at it.

"Where are these so-called friends of yours?" the tusked one asks while gnawing on his tail. "Why aren't they here supporting you when you are about to be eaten?"

"Maybe you'll find out if you let me finish the story."

"Please proceed."

CHAPTER NINETEEN

ANOTHER WEE KNOTHOLE

The youngers found the road, and farther along the road they found Shortcut shoveling snow away from Puff's tires.

"You youngers run along and find Blue," he said, panting and shoveling. "I'll get Puff out of this snowbank and be ready to hit the road when you return."

So the foursome set off across the meadow where they'd last seen the troll. The snow was melting and the sky brightening, revealing the troll's coffee table–sized footprints. Steam rose from the little rivulets that ran through the mossy ground and pooled in the depressions.

When the tracks ended abruptly, the youngers stopped, wondering what to do next.

"This is where they disappeared," Ren said. "It must be the border."

"Not even a dotted line on the ground!" Ant exclaimed.

"I think that only happens on maps," Boots said, then spat out some mealworms.

While they were talking, Tag began to have a feeling— she wouldn't have known how else to describe it. Have you ever caught a glimpse of something out of the corner of your eye? You turn, expecting to see something, only to discover that whatever you saw is gone—or maybe was never there. It was like that in a way. But instead of *seeing* something, she felt something on the corner of her face, like a little whisper or a kiss blown from someone who was not there. There was something so familiar about the feeling, but she couldn't put her finger on what it was.

When she felt the little spritz of air on her face again, she followed the flow of air until she discovered the weirdest thing: In the middle of the air, there was—somehow—a little round hole. Like a hole in a stocking. But even more like the knothole she'd pressed her eye against back home.

So, just as she used to do at home, she pressed her eye against it.

PART III
YET ANOTHER KINGDOM

CHAPTER TWENTY
A STRANGE BORDER

Looking through this strange little hole should have been like looking out the knothole in the wall at home, she thought. She assumed she would glimpse some other very different place.

Instead, it looked just the same as where she stood. There were the mountains, blue-black in the early morning light. There was the same dark-tinged heather. Nearby, a stream tumbled by, just like the one in this world. There was the same rocky ground patchworked with white moss, the same weathered stump spotted with lichen.

Then again, were there *eyes* in that stump? And was that stump not a stump at all? As she watched, the stump stretched and arms sprouted, then legs, and a weathered-looking creature appeared—a man with bark-like skin splotched with pale green lichen. But, no, as the little man approached, she could see that he was wearing a lichen-colored jacket, embroidered with infinitesimally fine gold threads. Soon he was so close that all she could see was one eye, looking into her eye. It so startled her that she yelped and backed away.

The youngers stared at the spot, watching as the little hole widened into a neatly shaped window, and a face appeared. Not an ordinary face, exactly, but it did have a nose and a mouth and two eyes that each seemed to look off in their own separate directions. The jacket sported a badge that Tag had not noticed before. A badge that said, "Border Patroll."

Tag wondered if that was a spelling error . . . or not.

Then the patroll set a placard on a suddenly materializing countertop that said *Customs and Immigration, Border Patroll.*

So, maybe not.

"Yes?" said the official, skewering her with his right eye while the left one gazed off into the distance.

"We'd like to pass over the border," Tag said. "We *need* to."

Now he shifted his gaze so the left eye looked at her and the right eye focused on the sky as if he were watching a comet. Tag couldn't help but glance upward to see what was going on up there.

"I'll need to see your passports," he said.

"Passports?" Tag directed her eyes back on the patroll. "Um . . . we don't have any."

Rolling his eyes in two different directions, he wordlessly shoved some papers at Tag, along with a pen.

CUSTOMS AND IMMIGRATION FORM

Name _____

Birth date _____

        Day   Month Year Century Epoch

Height _____ Weight _____ Number

of eyes _____ Number of heads _____

Extra limbs or other identifying features

_____

Species _____

Purpose of your visit (circle one): Business/
pleasure/troublemaking

Length of proposed stay _____

Address where you may be reached for further
harassment _____

Method of transportation (circle one): flying
ship/seven league boots/mortar and pestle/
broomstick

Occupation (circle one): rabbit herding/tying
things in knots/gold hoarding/rock throwing/
general troublemaking/specific troublemaking

Number of children _____

Number of children eaten _____

Number of children bewitched _____

Number of children terrorized _____

The youngers got only as far as "Species" before they had a question.

Tag carried the form back to the patroll. "What do you mean here, where it says 'species'?" She pointed to the question.

"Put down what species you are."

"You mean, like, human?"

"You mean to say you're Homo sapiens?" the patroll shrieked.

"Yes, of course. What else would we be?"

"Anything else!" The patroll snatched their papers away. "No, no, no, no, no. Humans are not allowed. Not allowed! Denied!" he said, stamping the form several times. "Go away!"

"What?"

"Are you deaf?" the patroll shouted, stamping their forms vigorously in rigorous succession. "Go away!" When Tag and the others did not go away, he stamped the forms again and shouted, "DENIED! No humans allowed over the border."

"Why not?"

"Why not? *Why not?* Don't get me started!" the patroll continued to shout. "The border is set up by nonhuman entities specifically to keep humans out. We welcome nonhuman types from all countries, continents, and every plane of existence. But not humans. No Homo sapiens."

"Why not?" Tag asked again.

"Again with the questions! I'll tell you why not," the patroll yelped. "We tried for a very long time to co-exist. We wanted to get along. But you humans really only value human life when it comes down to it, and it makes it very difficult. And I hate to say it, I really do, but you have been doing a terrible job of taking care of your plane of existence. Since we've kept humans out, things have improved. While humans have done their best to destroy the planet—*our* planet, I might add—we are working equally hard to preserve, at least to the extent to which we can, this one very narrow plane in which we exist. So, stay out!" The patroll slammed shut a sliding panel that Tag had not seen before, and the window suddenly disappeared.

Tag knocked on the panel. "But we aren't *those* humans! We're just youngers. We haven't destroyed anything and we don't plan to."

The panel slid open again and the face appeared. "Nobody *plans* to, do they? They just go blithely about their business, not wondering if they are contributing to the demise of the planet or not. These days, in order not to contribute, you have to really make an effort."

"Well, I don't *think* we're contributing," Tag said, although she was not sure. Maybe just their mere existence was part of the problem.

"Are you actively *not* contributing?" the patroll asked. "Hmmm?"

"Still, are we responsible for the problems our elders' elders created?" Tag asked.

"You might not be responsible, but it's still your problem. And you have to deal with it. And I don't know why I have to explain this to you!"

"But we *have* to get in. Our little dog—small, black-and-white, fluffy, long eyelashes, white eyebrows—was abducted! Kidnapped! By a troll! And is over *there*—on your side! Did you see them?"

"I can't keep track of all the trolls coming and going, not to mention who or what they've kidnapped." The patroll rolled one eye heavenward and the other one off to the side. "Look," he went on. "You don't want to get in here. No one on this side of the border likes human beings. Trust me on this. It would be safe to say that you and your kind would not be welcome here. Not at all. And I can't be responsible for your safety. Stay on your side and stay safe." He waved his hand and once again disappeared behind the invisible barrier.

Tag turned to the others. "Now what?"

"We'll just have to think of something else. Some other way," Ant said.

There wasn't any way to sneak through or climb over—how would they begin to find the edges of it? There was no use going around or tunneling under. There was really only one way: past the patroll.

"What does your book say to do?" Ren asked.

"Well . . ." Tag said. "I don't know about *pa*-trolls, but for trolls, it's best to try to trick them."

"How?" Boots asked, turning his head to spit out a couple of fungus beetles.

"What about a misguise?" asked Ren. "Or, er, a disguise?"

They looked at each other and instantly knew what they'd do.

In case the patroll was watching, the youngers trudged off as if they had given up. By now all the snow had melted, the walking was easier, and it didn't take them long to reach Shortcut, who was sitting on Puff's bumper, playing his guitar.

Once they explained to Shortcut about the border and their plan, he agreed to help however he could. They still had the flyer they'd found with the picture of the troll, and they studied the pictures and descriptions in Tag's book. Then, using Tag's fur coat, along with most of the other clothes in her rucksack, plus sticks, moss, heather, and lichen, not to mention some of the trash they'd collected, they created a troll costume. A *large* costume—big enough for four youngers. Boots on a pair of hastily put-together stilts, Ant on Boots's shoulders, Tag on Ant's shoulders, and Ren on Tag's shoulders.

"Boots, you are strong!" Ren crowed.

"Let's just hurry up," Boots said through gritted teeth and with some bug-spitting.

In the meantime, Shortcut had decked Puff out in a big green tarp, forming spikes along Puff's back with a long tail dragging behind. Then, with clouds of smoke issuing from Puff's "snout," they all made their way back to the border, Shortcut in the driver's seat and the youngers wobbling along, relying on Boots to do the walking.

Once they had finished squabbling over whose knees or elbows were poking whom, or who had perhaps been eating a little bit too much lately, and how they were ever going to find the window again, they all lumbered their way to the checkpoint. They also had to argue about what they were going to say once they got the attention of the patroll, and who was going to say it. Ren, though small, was loud and so was nominated.

Approaching the checkpoint, Ren bellowed out, "Troll coming through!"

The window slid open once again, and the patroll squinted out at them. "And what is that you have with you?" he asked, eyeing Puff skeptically.

"That is our pet dragon," Ren shouted.

Right on cue, a puff of smoke issued from the smoke-stack.

"Ah," said the patroll, seemingly satisfied with that. "What is the password?"

"There's a password?" Ren whispered to the others. "What do we do now?"

"Let's say we forgot," Tag whispered back.

"We forgot," Ren said loudly.

"*We?*" the patroll asked.

"Me and the dragon," Ren said.

"Then I have to ask you the security questions," the patroll said. "Question number one: The more you take, the more you leave behind."

"That's a security question?" Ren whined in a voice maybe sounding a little too nine-years-old.

"Take it or leave it," the patroll said.

"That's not even a question. It's a riddle," Ren complained.

"Remember what Austri said?" Tag whispered.

"Oh!" Ren cried, then, in a loud voice, proclaimed, "The more *footsteps* you take, the more you leave behind."

"Fine," the patroll said, a little disgruntled sounding. "Question number two: How far is it between east and west?"

"What was the other thing Austri said?" Ren whispered.

"The sun rises in the east, sets in the west, and it takes but one day," Boots said, accompanied by some gagging noises.

Ren repeated that (without the gagging) and added, "So, from east to west must be a day's journey!"

"I'll accept that," the patroll said. "Here is the last question: What am I thinking right now?"

"I suppose you're thinking it's a troll standing here before you," Ren said.

"Well, that's not wrong," the patroll said. "You may pass."

He waved his arm, the air shimmered, and the wobbly troll and its unusual pet stepped through the strangely wavering air.

"Oh ho," says one of my companions. "Now they are in for trouble."

The whole group laughs, an eerie assortment of creaking, groaning, whistling, and slobbering. One of them bends over to guffaw and a flap of plastic dangles dangerously close to the fire.

"Do you mind if I pull this plastic thing out of your fur?" I ask him. "I'm afraid it will catch fire."

"You don't like it?" he says. "I thought it gave me a certain je ne sais quoi. No? Fine, be my guest."

I pick the offending shred out of his fur, and with two fingers start pulling other bits of trash out of the tangles of the hair, fur, beard, tail, and foliage of which he is made. Roof shingles, parts of a kiddie pool, a tricycle tire, plastic ties, various bits of packaging, dental floss, and miscellaneous toys all come out of his furry self. I untangle an empty tube of lipstick from a beard, a rubber glove from underarm lichen, and a lot of sticky packing tape from his tail.

As I unwind a string from a deflated balloon that encircles one of the giant's ears, I continue the story.

CHAPTER TWENTY-ONE

THE SILVER FOREST

Once they were out of sight of the patroll, they all tumbled off one another's shoulders, threw off their troll disguise, and pulled the long green tarp off Puff. All these things were stowed on board the bus. Then they looked around, hoping that the way they should go would reveal itself.

It did not take long to see which way to go. The morning sun illuminated a wide plain dotted with pale rocks and clumps of white lichen and, rising in the distance, the mountains. The sun had painted the outlines of the mountains and was busy coloring them in with a deep lavender, turning to blue.

"The mountains!" they exclaimed. "Turning blue. We better hurry!"

Just as they had forgotten the advice of the first sister, the youngers forgot the advice of the second sister. They all piled into the bus and instead of keeping the sun over their right shoulders, Shortcut aimed straight for the mountains, with the sun against their backs.

As morning turned to afternoon, they noticed something else rising out of the plain. Something that sparkled in the sunlight. A kind of forest. A very shiny, glittery forest. They had watched its sparkle grow brighter and brighter as they approached down the bumpy road. Now, in the slanted afternoon light, the trunks of the trees seemed to glisten, and the leaves as they twisted in the breeze glittered like silver jewelry.

It was late in the day by the time they reached a pair of gates upon which a flyer was posted. Shortcut let the bus idle while the youngers stepped outside to read it.

> "WARNING." PRIVATe DOMAne.
> DO NOT BRaKe A BRANCH!
> Nor A TWIGG! NOR lET YOUR
> BREATH RUSSel A LEAF! AT PERILL
> OF YOUR LYFE."
> Your's Trully,
> The proprietor

"That doesn't sound very friendly," Ant said.

"Well, kids," Shortcut said, "we are in a pickle. Well, not a literal pickle, but a kind of figurative pickle. I'm not sure how to tell you this, but I don't think Puff can go along that narrow lane without breaking off leaves or twigs or even whole branches."

"What if . . ." Ant said, "you drive very slowly, while we carefully move aside any branches that might be in the way?"

"Ren in the front," Boots said. "Ant and Tag on either side." He paused to spit out a few cockroaches. "I'll go up on the hood and the roof."

"We'll have to be very careful not to break off any leaves ourselves!" Ren said.

Boots opened the gates and the youngers took their positions. Shortcut steered Puff slowly down the narrow lane while the others trotted ahead to move branches. Ren used the harpoon to lift them aside. Boots pranced back and forth from the hood to the roof, lifting branches up and out of the way.

In this way they picked their way through the forest, bending and ducking and weaving, trying to avoid touching the leaves. It was all a bit of a delicate dance, and the youngers were so concentrated on their task that they barely noticed the beauty of the leaves and the trees that surrounded them. But then, when the last rays of the setting sun struck the leaves and set them glimmering, Tag felt an overwhelming desire to touch one of them.

"Do you think these are the leaves that blow into our town when youngers are windswept?" she asked, reaching up to touch a leaf. "Do you ever wonder why our elders love these leaves more than they love—" With a tiny snap, the leaf came off in her hand.

At the same time, the sun slipped over the horizon, the light dimmed, the leaves lost their luster, and Puff coughed, sputtered, and conked out.

Then, for a moment, silence. Except for a deep, faraway rumble. Thunder? Or . . . something else?

Shortcut pulled the door open and yelled, "Get in!"

Ant and Tag dashed around and clambered inside. Boots slithered off the roof and darted into the bus.

"Tykes, we are in a pickle," Shortcut said. "Worse than a pickle. We are in a cauldron of pickle relish. Puff is out of fuel. And we are in a forest where we can't break a leaf or a twig . . ."

All eyes went to the leaf in Tag's hand, glimmering in the last light of day. Or all eyes except one pair.

"Where is Ren?" Tag asked.

There was a long, low roll of thunder that rattled the bus's windows. The ground shook. Leaves quivered. Puff rocked.

"Ren is outside!" Shortcut said, pointing to Ren standing on the hood, harpoon raised.

Through the forest came the heavy, booming thud of footfall and the sound of trees snapping and cracking.

Something was coming. Something very large.

CHAPTER TWENTY-TWO
THE TROLL

The troll was enormous, covered in mossy fur, dotted here and there with mushrooms and shelf fungi. His head, brushing the treetops, had a nose like a tree stump, and his forehead was like a rocky crag overhanging a single glowing eye. His long beard was composed mostly of lichen but also bits of . . . was that plastic? Tattered plastic fluttered like ribbons from his fur. Hundreds or maybe even thousands of tiny plastic bits twinkled almost like glitter or sequins among the dark moss and fur that made up his torso. A plastic bag, snagged on a small tree growing out of his head, inflated and deflated in the breeze.

Under one arm he carried a small black-and-white dog, ears flattened in misery.

"Who dares touch my trees?" the giant roared, causing the leaves to rattle on the branches.

"Shhh!" Ren said to him. "Don't wake the dragon."

"What dragon?" rumbled the troll, twisting his huge, shaggy head to look behind him.

"This big orange dragon," Ren piped, pointing at Puff with the harpoon.

"This is dragon?" the troll roared, laying a paw on the roof, which jostled the bus and everyone inside.

"Don't touch!" Ren commanded. "You'll wake her, and you don't want to do that or she will swallow you like she swallowed my friends."

The rest of the crew was cowering inside, listening to this exchange through an open window. Tag wished she was brave enough to go outside and help Ren, but she was not.

"Oh," said the troll, peeking through the window at the others. "Is that why they're in there?"

A line of tiny red ants marched down Boots's chin as he stared, open-mouthed and speechless, at the giant.

"I *fight* dragon," the troll said. His breath washed over Tag and the others, a mix of dead fish, sour milk, and rotten eggs.

"Are you sure?" Ren said, standing with hands on hips and feet planted far apart. "The dragon has already swallowed most of us. Except me, of course. And we are mighty warriors ourselves. Of course, I'm the mightiest."

"You?" the troll laughed so hard that putrid green drool rolled off his lip and dribbled down his belly.

"You don't believe me? Watch this." Ren opened a fist to show what looked like a round, white stone. "I'll squeeze this stone 'til it bleeds!"

The giant's eyes shifted under his heavy brow. He squinted, watching as Ren squeezed the thing until a milky liquid dripped from it.

The other youngers stared out the window at the contest.

"Is that what I think it is?" Ant whispered. "You mean that little imp still had some goat cheese after all this time?"

"Shhh!" Tag hushed him.

Ren had tossed away the now-squished lump of cheese and was saying to the troll, "Now give us our dog or I'll squeeze *you* like I squeezed that stone."

"You squeeze stone," he said. "I squeeze *you*!" In a swift and unexpected move, he scooped up Ren in his free fist.

Tag's breath left her body in the rush of a single word: "NO!" She rocketed off the bus and, with a flying leap, grabbed hold of the troll's long beard.

"Let go of Ren!" she cried, dangling from his beard as if from the attic door.

The troll shook his head, flinging Tag from side to side. "Let go, pest!" he roared.

"Make me!" Tag yelled.

The troll looked at his two paws, both occupied, one clasping a tiny younger, the other a tiny dog.

"You'll have to set at least one of those two down to do it," Tag taunted.

The troll set Ren on the hood and used that hand to swipe at Tag. But Tag used her feet to push off his belly, as if off a mountain, and swung away from his swiping paw each time it came at her, so that finally he had to set the dog down, too.

Blue dashed lickety-split, tail between her legs, onto the bus and crawled under a throw rug.

The troll grabbed Tag with two hands, yanked her off his beard, and tossed her aside with disgust.

"Listen," Ren said, addressing the giant from the hood of the bus. "We don't want to harm you." The troll turned his stunned eye in that direction. "It would really be best if the dragon doesn't wake up while you're here. Or wake up in your forest, for that matter, for she's a fire breather. If you don't believe me, peek into that nostril there." Ren pointed the harpoon at the firebox in the back of the bus.

The troll lifted the lid of the firebox with one finger, and a puff of smoke billowed out. He quickly replaced the lid.

"When she wakes up, she starts breathing fire like mad," Ren said, "and she's likely to burn your forest down, and you with it!"

"My forest! What should I do?" the troll whined.

"If you push her out of here—very gently—and into a nice, regular forest with trees made of regular wood, you might escape with your miserable life," Ren said. "Even though you're a clay-brained oaf, you must push very, very gently, so as not to wake her. Wait 'til I give you the signal."

The troll went round to the back of the bus while Tag climbed inside.

"Come inside!" Tag whispered to Ren.

Ren seemed not to have heard, balancing on the hood as if ensconced on the bow of a whaleship. When Ren gave the signal, Shortcut, with trembling fingers, shifted the bus into neutral.

The troll plunked his paws down on the bus, *Thunk, thunk*, making it rock and sway.

"In the name of gudgeons and ginger cakes!" Ren hollered. "*Gently!*"

Grunting and groaning, the troll proceeded to push, with Ren encouraging him like an old sea captain might.

"Easy now, easy; don't be in a hurry," Ren crooned. "Softly, softly! That's it—that's it! The devil fetch you, you piratical cutthroat—*gently!*" The orange beast creaked as it rocked along the road. Inside, the youngers barely breathed while Shortcut gripped the wheel. Ren clutched the harpoon in both hands, as if expecting a whale to emerge at any moment. All the while, Puff rolled silently through the forest, illuminated by the light of the troll's glowing eye.

At the end of the lane and on the other side of a gate, they were deposited in a wooded glen of normal trees growing normal leaves.

There was a moment when they all waited, holding their breath, wondering what would happen next. Should they say thank you, Tag wondered? Maybe it was best to stay quiet and hope the troll would just move on.

And so he seemed to do. Turning with a grunt, he began to shuffle away.

Inside Puff, everyone let out their breath, feeling as though they'd been holding it forever.

Who knows what seized Ren at that moment? Perhaps it was the sight of the troll's enormous backside and the fine target it made, compounded by Ren's desire for revenge. Aiming the harpoon at the retreating troll, Ren hollered, "Your hour is at hand, fiend! Fear my wrath and my lance!"

"No, Ren, no!" Tag shouted.

"Don't do it!" said Ant.

"Noooo!" they all hollered as the harpoon was released and spun through the air, launched straight at the troll's ample rear end.

With a thunderous roar, the troll stopped. Then he slowly turned to look behind him. Turning and turning, he eyed the harpoon protruding from his hind end like a dog suddenly aware of its tail.

But when the troll's gaze fell on Ren, who was still standing on the hood of the bus, his single eye turned a fiery sunset red. With a snort, he charged straight for the bus, giving Puff a swift kick before scooping both harpoon and harpooner into his paws. Then, without a backward glance, he loped off into the forest with the loudly cursing Ren in his fist.

"They should have turned back instead of going through that troll's forest," says my tusked companion when I get up to throw another stick on the fire. "These young humans really make things hard for themselves. Why don't they give up?"

"Why work so hard?" says the old grizzled graybeard.

"Well," I tell them, "I know at least one old woman who will tell you that most things worth doing are at least a little bit difficult."

"That's old people for you," says the rumbly voice on the far side of the fire. "They just know too much. It's better not to know so much. It's better to only know what you want to know and leave it at that."

"What I want to know is are those coals nearly ready?" says the head under the arm. "I am hungry!" Drool glistens down her chin and drips onto the hand that holds her head.

"Soon, drooly," old graybeard says. "First let us find out what happened next." He turns toward me and commands, "Go on."

CHAPTER TWENTY-THREE
STYMIED

A fter them!" Boots shouted at Shortcut, beetles and fireflies spraying from his mouth.

"Can't," Shortcut said. "Puff is plum out of fuel. There's no more road." He gestured at the road ahead, which quickly shrank to a footpath. "You better go on foot. I'll refuel and be ready whenever you come back."

The youngers wasted no time. They scrambled down the stairs and out into the night, following the sounds of the troll crashing through the trees and Ren's salty curses. Blue trotted along behind, staying uncharacteristically quiet.

For a while, that was all they needed to keep up, but the troll's huge stride carried him and his captive swiftly away. It wasn't long before the youngers lost him, and with him, Ren.

"And it's all my fault!" Tag cried.

"No," said Ant, "Ren is the one who threw that harpoon."

But Tag couldn't help thinking that if she hadn't

touched the silver leaf, Ren would still be with them. And if she hadn't slept outside, Blue wouldn't have been stolen. And if she hadn't paused when the wind came, Finn wouldn't have been windswept. Everything seemed to be her fault. And now it was too dark to go anywhere.

"What do we do now?" Boots asked, coughing out a handful of spiders. He looked around as if waiting for an answer, but Ren, the voice of reason, was gone. "I suppose Ren would say that we have to wait until morning when we can pick up the trail again."

There was no point in going back to the bus. They would only lose the ground they'd gained. So, Ant made a little fire. They laid the tablecloth and ate a meager meal. And Boots, a few moths fluttering out of his mouth as soon as he opened it, asked Tag to read a story.

"Really?" she said. "Now?"

"Yes, now," Ant said. "Now is exactly when we need a story."

Tag opened the book and, by the light of the fire, read the first story that she came to: "The Frog Prince."

Between the holes, Tag pieced together the story of a princess who lost her golden ball in a pond and a frog who got it back for her on the condition that she take him home and let him eat from her plate and sleep in her bed. She promised these things but then didn't take the frog home, after all.

"*The next day,*" Tag read, "*the princess had just sat down to dinner when who should come, splish, splash, splish, splash, up the marble staircase, but the frog, demanding to sit at the table and eat from her plate and sleep in her bed.*

"*He climbed up on the table and ate right off her plate, then demanded the princess carry him to her room. But when he said to put her on the bed, the princess became so annoyed, she picked up the frog and threw him against the wall with all her might!*"

At this juncture in the story, Ant said, "Harsh!" and Boots made a face.

"*Now you'll get your rest, you disgusting frog!*'" Tag went on.

"She's nasty!" Boots said, "and so are these," he added as he picked box elder bugs out of his mouth.

"*When the frog fell to the ground, he was no longer a frog but a prince with beautiful, bright eyes. At her father's bidding, he became her dear companion and husband.*"

"After that kind of abuse, he actually marries her?" Ant said. "And that's the end?"

"Not quite," Tag said, reading on. "*The next day a coach drove up and on the back of the coach stood Faithful Heinrich, the servant of the young prince. He had been so saddened by the transformation of his master into a frog (by a wicked witch) that three hoops had been placed around his chest to keep his heart from bursting with pain and sorrow. The princess and the young prince got into the carriage and Faithful Heinrich took his place in the rear. When the coach had gone some distance, the prince heard a noise behind him, as if something had broken. He turned around and cried out, 'Heinrich, the coach is falling apart.'*

"'No, my lord, it's not the coach, but a hoop from around my heart which was in sheer pain when you were down in the spring, living there as a frog.'

"Two more times the prince heard the cracking noise and he was sure the coach was falling apart. But it was only the sound of the hoops breaking from around Faithful Heinrich's chest, for his master had been set free and he was happy."

"That's the end," Tag finished.

"Well maybe the prince ought to have married good old Faithful Heinrich," Ant said. "He loved the prince even when he was a frog. Which is more than the princess ever did."

Boots and Tag agreed that would have been a better match. And they agreed that fairy tales were strange. "Maybe these stories do teach us the wrong message," Ant said, "and that's why we aren't supposed to read them."

"Even if they do, I feel like I can handle it," Boots said, spitting a tree frog into his hand. "I mean, I can think for myself. Make my own judgment." He carefully set the little frog on the ground. "Even if they do have questionable values or messages or whatever, can't we figure that out for ourselves?"

Ant nodded, agreeing. "Just because we're young doesn't mean we're ignorant!"

Tag nodded, but what she was really thinking about was her mother's stiff, black dress. Maybe that tight bodice, like Faithful Heinrich's iron bands, was the only thing that kept her heart from breaking. For the first time, she understood why her mother wore that dress with its metal stays circling her heart. Tag wished she had something wrapped around her *own* chest to keep her heart from breaking.

CHAPTER TWENTY-FOUR

A SEEMINGLY TRANQUIL LAKE

All the next day, they followed the troll's big footprints, trying as best they could to catch up.

"The troll must have stopped to take shelter somewhere," Tag said. "Trolls can't be out in the daytime."

"Why not?" Ant asked.

"If sunlight hits them, they turn to stone," Tag explained.

"That is something I'd like to see," Boots said, spitting out ants like watermelon seeds.

The table-sized footprints led to the edge of a big lake where, on the shore, broken in half, lay Ren's harpoon.

Ant sadly picked it up and tried to fit it together.

"Do you think they went across the lake?" Boots asked, absentmindedly pulling an earthworm from between his teeth.

"They must have," Tag said. "There are no footprints leading anywhere else, and if the troll was heading toward the mountains like Austri said . . . well, look!" On the other side of the lake, the mountains rose straight out of the water, appearing queasily regal in bruised-looking yellow and purple.

Luckily, there was a boat sitting at the water's edge, as if waiting for them. It was even outfitted with oars.

"Do you think it's safe?" Tag wondered.

"Look at the lake!" Boots said, while a leech oozed out of the corner of his mouth. The lake was a mirror, as blue as the sky, so still that the reflection of the mountains seemed as real as the mountains themselves. Not a puff of wind.

So they shoved the boat in the water and climbed in, setting Blue on the bottom of the boat. She cast Tag a doubtful look. And perhaps she was right to be skeptical, for of course not one of them had ever rowed a boat before—when would they have had the opportunity to do that?

Naturally, the rowing didn't go smoothly at first. Boots, the strongest of them, was at the oars while Ant and Tag shouted orders and advice.

"Watch out for that lily pad!"

"Pull harder with the other oar!"

First they went in a big circle and then in a wobbly zigzag that went nowhere. The boat seemed to groan and sigh with each wrong turn. But soon enough Boots got the hang of it and began to make steady progress toward the opposite shore.

"Tell us a story, Tag," Ant said.

"I don't feel like telling a story," Tag said. "Why don't you tell one?"

"Fine," Ant said, and he began:

"Once upon a time not long ago, there was a man and a woman who had too many offspring and there was not enough food for them, so they took the three youngest and left them in a wood. The parents went back the next day and found silver leaves scattered over the ground where they'd left their little ones. But the little ones were gone. So they collected the leaves for themselves, and after that there was food in the house—at least for a while. But what became of the little ones I don't know, because I am the oldest and my parents kept me at home. Maybe because I was old enough to do some work."

"What?" Tag said. "Is this your real story? Did that really happen to you?"

"Your parents really left your siblings in the forest?" Boots said, pausing in his rowing to pick a daddy longlegs out of his mouth. "And they were windswept?"

Ant nodded and went on. "We were not allowed to speak of our siblings again," Ant said. "It was as if they had never existed. And after that I started eating, eating everything I could find, afraid that if my parents put me out, I would starve. Afraid that I might someday have to survive for a long time Outside by myself. Well, to be honest, I don't really know why I eat all the time and why I am willing to eat things that no one else will.

"I had always hoped that the little tykes would just walk into the house one day, telling of their adventures. But no. It's been too long. We two older ones vowed to each other that we would someday try to find them, hoping they were still alive. Whichever one of us had the chance. And that was me."

"I hope we find them, Ant," Tag whispered.

"We will," Boots grunted, not bothering with whatever was slithering out of his mouth. He was pulling hard on the oars; the wind had freshened.

Tag glanced up to see that clouds had covered the sun, and the placid water had turned to choppy waves. Boots, back to the wind, rowed on. The choppy water next turned to angry waves, fiercely trying to push them backward. When Boots let up for an instant, the boat bobbed helplessly.

"Oof!" the boat seemed to say as the bow slammed into a wave. "Ow!" it barked as it came down hard over the next wave.

The little rowboat couldn't seem to make any forward progress, and Boots struggled just to keep it pointed into the wind and waves.

Ant and Tag each grabbed an oar and tried to help Boots row, but it was hopeless. They couldn't go forward, and now water was sloshing over the bow, pooling around their feet. Blue lifted first one paw out of the water and then the other, as if she might keep her paws dry that way.

"What should we do?" Tag shouted over the wind.

The wind decided for them. It spun their little boat sideways to the waves, so it pitched and heaved. With each rolling wave, water sloshed over the side, collecting on the bottom. Blue stood shivering, looking ragged and miserable as the water crept up her legs to her belly.

"Start bailing!" Tag yelled. First she used the saucepan to ladle water out of the boat. Ant used the mugs, tossing the water into the lake only to have most of it flung back into the boat by the wind. Then Tag thought of the rucksack. Maybe it could hold all the water the way it had held all the clothes in her escape rope. She slid out the book of fairy tales and set it on the seat next to her, then used the empty rucksack to scoop and heft and dump.

With the cold spray slapping her face and soaking her clothes, and the little boat lurching over the waves, Tag found the whole experience simultaneously exhilarating and terrifying. Exhilarating because for once she felt she was not at the utter mercy of the wind but was actually doing something about it. Terrifying because the wind and water seemed to be getting the upper hand.

Soon there was so much water in the boat that Blue had to dog-paddle to stay afloat. Even the rucksack could not hold enough of it. The youngers' arms were sore and tired from the constant and futile effort of shoveling water out of the boat. The waves had only grown higher and the wind angrier.

Tag looked out to see an enormous wave, bigger than all the others. As it rolled toward them, it appeared as big as a watery giant who, with watery hands, upended their boat, tipping them all into the lake.

———○———

Yet another world, Tag thought, once she had stopped tumbling and began sinking into a strangely still and quiet underwater kingdom. As different from above the water as the Outside was from the inside. The roar of the wind, the tumult of the waves, all of that was somewhere else.

In the story of the three windswept princesses, the soldier had to pass through water and fire before he could reach the land where the girls were held captive. Although she was passing through water, Tag did not think it would soon mean she'd be rescuing her sisters. In fact, as she sank down and down, she supposed this meant she would not ever rescue anybody, even herself. She didn't know how to swim! How would she ever have learned? Her comrades would not know either, she knew, but she hoped they were faring better than she was. She turned her head, looking for them, but unless they had dissolved into bubbles, she didn't see anyone.

And she didn't even know which way to try to point herself. Then, above her head, there was the book, floating open, its pages wafting in the water like strands of hair. What if the words are being washed away, she thought. Get the book!

It took only the kicking of her feet to find herself rising, up and up, until her hands grabbed the book, and her head broke the surface, where she took a deep, sputtering breath. There was Blue Tooth, dog-paddling away. And there were the others, thrashing like she was, toward the not-too-distant shore.

Later, after they had all dragged themselves out of the lake onto the same shore they had left hours earlier, and after they'd hauled the boat up on land (and watched in amazement as it shook itself dry and trundled off into the underbrush), and after they'd draped their wet clothes and wet book over the shrubs and branches to dry, and after Boots had spit out mouthful after mouthful of water bugs, minnows, and crayfish, and after Blue had shaken herself dry for the umpteenth time, they collapsed under a large tree with spreading branches.

Most of the leaves had fallen among the logs and boulders and lumps of earth that seemed to have arranged themselves for the youngers' benefit. There was a bench-like log and lumpy roots and mossy hillocks placed in convenient places for them to sit and rest. Somewhere high in the tree above them, birds poured out songs of trills and missed notes, mixed in with a couple of raspy croaks.

As darkness fell, Ant gathered twigs and sticks for a fire. Boots, ignoring one last crayfish that spurted out of his mouth, said, "Let's have a story?" And Blue, who was still a little damp, curled up on Tag's lap and peered at her as if to say, "Yes, a story."

Tag shifted on the lump of earth upon which she had been sitting, trying to get more comfortable, when the lump of earth shifted, as if to make *itself* more comfortable. She was too tired to take much notice of it.

While Ant worked at getting a fire going—no small feat with wet matches—Tag carefully pulled apart the sodden, stuck-together pages of her book, trying to decide on a story.

"I like the one where the strange little Rumple-what's-his-name tears himself in two," said Boots, coughing up a few mayflies.

"You've got to admit, some of the stories are pretty violent," Ant observed. "Even cruel. Like making an evil queen dance in red hot shoes until she falls down dead."

"Well, she was evil. She deserved it," Boots said. He stared cross-eyed down at a water beetle marooned on his tongue.

"Did she?" Ant wondered. "I mean, that's torture, isn't it? And we don't think torture is all right, no matter how bad the person might be. They're still a human being."

"Maybe they believed torture was okay in the Other Times—or whenever fairy tales were written," Boots said, while an inchworm inched its way out of his mouth.

"Well, they believed in stereotypes and other bad stuff that they put in the stories, too," Ant said. "The overly cruel punishments, princesses waiting to be rescued by princes, and things like that. Maybe that's why the Powers-That-Be don't want us to read these stories. We have moved beyond those things and know better."

Boots agreed, saying, "People in the Other Times were ignorant and prejudiced in a way we are not. We don't believe in wrong things anymore."

Tag wondered. *Were* they so enlightened? Her brief sojourn in the underwater world made her wonder if there might be things they just didn't know or hadn't learned yet. Up until the moment the boat tipped, she'd never imagined how different it might be underwater. Life might be like that. Indeed, it certainly seemed to be so far! There was always something more to know. Something or someone new to encounter. New ideas to try to understand. It seemed you could never run out of things to learn. And maybe there were prejudices and stereotypes or just accepted ways of thinking that were not yet understood, simply because . . . well, if you spend your whole life on top of the water, how can you know that there's a whole different world *under*water?

———○———

But before she could say anything about her thoughts, they were interrupted by a loud roar and an enormous voice hollering, "My foot is on fire!"

The ground began to stretch, and the whole collection of earth and rock and shrubs and moss assembled itself into a very large being that slowly rose, towering above them, stumbled the few steps to the lake, and plunged its flaming foot into the water.

The youngers were paralyzed with what Ren might have called "terrification." When Tag had collected herself, she looked the monster up and down, noticing the small tree growing out of his head, upon which fluttered a plastic grocery bag. "I recognize that plastic bag," she said.

Whimpering, the troll clutched his burnt foot in both paws, then turned and cast his single eye's searchlight-like beam over them.

The youngers tried to back up. Blue squirmed in Tag's arms.

"YOU!" the troll bellowed, hopping toward them on one foot. "You set my foot on fire!"

"We didn't know it was your foot," Tag said, her voice trembling, "or we never would have done such a thing. Please accept our apologies."

The troll's one eye squinted at them, and Tag forced herself to look into the glowing orb, crisscrossed with red veins. "We are here to get our friend, Ren," she said, as calmly as she could manage.

"Ah, yes, your little friend is in here somewhere," the troll said, rustling the tree branches.

"Ren is in the tree?" Tag asked, tipping her head back to look at the branches he was shaking. Even in the moonlight, it was obvious there wasn't a human person in the tree. The only thing to be seen, besides the bare branches, were roosting birds. Of those, there were quite a number.

"There are just birds up there," Ant pointed out.

"Correct," the troll agreed.

Peering into the branches, Tag marveled to see so many kinds and sizes of birds chirping, squawking, and trilling from seemingly every branch. Yellow finches, blue jays, iridescent hummingbirds, a bright red cardinal, and at the topmost branch, a big, black raven swayed back and forth, back and forth.

"I got worn out from that little one's curses. I'd rather listen to birds," the troll explained. "And they are pretty."

Ant whispered to the others, "Is he saying that one of those birds is Ren?"

The answer came in a song full of missed notes, strangely loopy trills, and if a bird could hurl oaths, this one was doing it.

"That's Ren," Boots said, coughing a few beetles into his hand.

"That's *a* wren," the troll said, chortling. "But all this has made me very hungry," he went on. "And you"—he paused to count—"one, two . . . well, however many of you there are, look *delicious!*"

The surrounding hills reverberated with his shout. In a surprisingly swift move, the giant scooped up Tag and Boots, one in each hand, licked his lips, opened his cavernous mouth, which was large enough to accommodate a hibernating bear, and popped the two of them inside.

CHAPTER TWENTY-FIVE
THE EATING MATCH

Nothing, Tag thought, *nothing* could be as utterly disgusting as the inside of a troll's mouth: the moldy teeth, the slime-covered tongue, the deep, dark, endless chute of his throat. She squeezed her eyes shut for the inevitable when she heard a distant voice—so far away as to possibly be in her imagination—saying, "I'm hungry, too."

The troll dropped his jaw and said, "Huh?"

Opening her eyes, Tag could see Ant through the troll's open mouth, standing on the ground, his hands on his hips.

"I repeat: I'm hungry, too. I propose a contest," Ant said with head tipped back to look at the troll. "An eating match. But if you want to participate, you have to take those youngers out of your mouth."

"Huh?" the troll said, his mouth still hanging open.

"We must both eat the same things—that's the rules," Ant said. "Put those two down."

With four stubby fingers, the troll withdrew Tag and Boots from his mouth and set them on the ground.

"Here's the wager," Ant went on, as Tag and Boots wiped the slime off themselves. "If I win, you let Ren go and don't eat us. And if you win, well, I guess you get to do whatever you want."

"But what are we to eat?" the troll asked. "If not you?"

"I'll take care of that," said Ant. "You provide the table and chairs."

Without a word, the troll pulled up a big stump and set it down between them. Two more stumps, one big and one small, he pulled up and plunked down on either side of the table. While he was busy with that, Ant pulled the tablecloth from Tag's rucksack. Then Boots hoisted Ant up onto the skinnier of the stumps.

"Now for the meal," Ant said, shaking out the tablecloth and saying, "Cloth, spread thyself!"

Boots and Tag stood back—*well* back—wondering what, if anything, the cloth could provide in this rocky moor?

Nothing, it seemed.

"That cloth is busted," said the troll, while folding his mammoth self onto his own sturdy stump.

"It's a *vintage* tablecloth," Ant said. "Give it time."

Sure enough, not instantly, but little by little, dishes began to appear. First the dish, then the food inside it. A chafing dish gradually filled with steaming porridge, a pitcher with cream, a bowl with strawberries.

A silver platter piled up with turkey legs, then sliced roast beef.

A casserole dish slowly filled with something vaguely unidentifiable but delicious smelling.

Soup showed up in a tarnished tureen.

A crock produced a hearty stew.

Tea arrived steaming in a copper teakettle.

Ant and the troll set to the food with great appetite, and soon the only sounds were of chewing and chomping and slurping and grunting and belching. And possibly the escape of other gases.

The troll shoved baked apples into his mouth while slurping up mutton broth at the same time. Ant set to work diligently but politely, using the silverware the tablecloth had provided in a mannerly way.

When the troll was distracted by a leg of lamb, Tag set her rucksack on Ant's lap. "When you can eat no more," she whispered, "just shovel the food into it."

Ant nodded and set into some crunchy little biscuits and soft cakes. Thick slices of bread with slabs of butter. Thinly sliced ham and salami. Tender green peas and steamed young carrots. A heaping pile of mashed potatoes covered with rich gravy.

Each time the food on the tablecloth ran out, it would fill again.

Oat cakes and seed bread. Roast game hen and haunch

of venison, dandelion greens, meat pies, stewed fruit and custards, boiled mutton and currant jelly, oyster pie and stewed liver, cold tongue, calf's head.

After the two eaters had been chomping away for a couple of hours, the dishes began arriving with a groan. A few fizzling sparks and smoke rose from the tablecloth, as if the effort of producing all that food had been too much for it. The food, too, began to take a little longer to appear, and when it did, it was not always ready for consumption.

The salad was wilted, the bread doughy and gooey, soufflés fallen. A few dozen raw eggs appeared in a bowl—unfazed, the troll tipped up the bowl and downed its contents without hesitation.

A live chicken ran around the tablecloth clucking madly. The troll reached for it, but the others shooed it away before he could devour it, too.

A few snapping sparks rose from the empty gravy boat as it tried, and failed, to fill. Empty platters stayed empty. A crock offered nothing but crumbs.

What if the food ran out before the troll was full? Tag wondered, her heart flopping about like a fish in the bottom of a boat.

But then the troll's eye began to roll around in his head, eyelid fluttering. He emitted one long, powerful groan and keeled over, falling off his chair and onto the ground, out cold.

Ant seemed perfectly fine. He wiped his mouth on the edge of the tablecloth, stood up, took a deep breath, and said, "What a fine meal!"

The tablecloth emitted a fizz, a crackle, and a wisp of smoke, then lay quite still.

"The tablecloth has given its all," Ant said, giving it a little bow. "One can ask for nothing greater."

Tag and Boots broke into spontaneous applause for Ant and for the tablecloth that had served them so well. Now it lay limp, its edges frayed with exhaustion.

Boots spat out a few spiders, and asked Ant, "How did you manage to eat all that?"

"I didn't!" Ant said. "Well, that is, I ate quite a bit, but when I couldn't eat anymore, I just shoveled the food into Tag's rucksack."

"But that was sooo much food!" Boots said, picking one last spider out of his teeth.

"I know!" Ant said. "But the rucksack never seemed to fill up!"

"How did you know the tablecloth would come through for you?" Tag asked.

"Sometimes," Ant said, "you just have to have a little faith."

Their celebration was interrupted by angry chirping and so much ruffling of feathers that a little flurry of them drifted down from the treetop.

"Ren!" Tag said, "why don't you come down here?"

The answer came in a series of shrill whistles and trills.

"Why isn't Ren joining us?" Ant wondered.

The trills and whistles grew louder, more insistent, and, frankly, more profane.

Ant squinted up into the tree. The moon had set but the birds were visible—dark shapes against the milky light of predawn. "Maybe Ren doesn't know how to fly," he suggested.

The tree stretched up and up, long and straight, with branches that did not begin until over their heads. Gazing up, Tag wondered aloud, "What are we going to do?"

But Boots was already shimmying up the trunk. Soon he had reached the first branches. "There are a lot of birds up here," he called down to them, while June bugs buzzed out of his mouth. "They can't fly, because they're all tied to branches!"

Tag shook her fist at the downed troll and said through gritted teeth, "Louse!"

Ant laughed and said Ren would have come up with a better insult than that.

In response, the wren overhead launched a full-scale, semi-musical attack, hitting a series of notes likely never heard in the natural world before or since.

"What should I do?" Boots said from his perch in the tree.

"Untie all of them!" Tag shouted up at him.

"Don't fall out of the tree!" Ant advised.

"And hurry," Tag said, "before this brute wakes up with a stomachache."

Boots worked his way up branch by branch, tiptoeing carefully out on precarious limbs or sometimes stretching himself full-length to reach a robin or a jay or a phoebe tied to outlying twigs.

Each time a bird was released, it offered up a full-throated song of thanks so that soon the tree was filled with birdsong and the flutter of wings and, in the light of the coming dawn, the flash of color.

From the wren's tether, it continued to blast out what surely must have been oaths and curses, urging Boots along with the strongest possible language. Undeterred, he just kept swinging from one limb to the next, hanging by one hand while freeing a bird with the other.

Tag watched with a mix of wonder and anxiety. For one thing, she noticed with increasing alarm that the troll was starting to stir.

"Hurry!" Tag, bouncing on her toes, shouted up to Boots. "But, also, be careful!" Her eyes drifted to the very top of the tree, where a glossy raven calmly watched Boots's progress upward. Every so often the bird pecked at its foot, or at whatever kept it tied to the branch.

Next, Boots edged out to the wren, who had been tied to a tiny twig.

"I can't reach you," he said. "Can you come closer to me?" Whenever Boots spoke, the entire flock of birds swirled around his head, in hopes of snagging the bugs, worms, or tasty insects that escaped his mouth.

The wren hopped along the branch toward Boots, then stopped and tugged at one leg, unable to go any farther. Boots gritted his teeth and stretched out as long as his lanky self would go, just far enough to snap the twig to which the wren was tied.

Tag watched as the tiny bird that was Ren lifted into the air and wobbled about ungracefully, then flitted and fluttered like a drunken butterfly.

"One more, Boots," Tag called. "At the very top of the tree. The raven."

Boots tipped his head back and let out a groan. The branches grew thinner the farther up the tree he went. Even the weight of the raven caused the branch to sway and bob.

The big, dark-colored bird tilted its head to give Boots a one-eyed stare. Its feathered throat ruffled in the wind.

"I don't know . . ." Boots called out, releasing a small squadron of dragonflies, which, when they got close enough, were snapped up by the raven. "That is a very large bird. And the branches are very thin."

"You can't just leave him there," Tag shouted, while trying to avoid the arms and legs of the troll, who was clearly rousing. "But hurry!" she squeaked.

Boots continued his upward climb. The branches barely supported the bird. How would a lanky boy in oversize boots fare?

"Faster, Boots!" Tag squawked, clamoring over a huge leg. She had to keep moving to avoid the now thrashing limbs of the giant.

High in the tree, the branch bent as Boots inched farther out onto it.

With a tremendous yawn, the troll sat up and blinked open his eye. At the same time the branch above him cracked and gave way.

Up into the air went the raven with a startled whoosh of wings, while Boots came plummeting down, landing with a thud and a loud "Oof!" right on top of the troll's head.

A squadron of wasps streamed out of Boots's mouth straight into the troll's open one.

Coughing and gagging, the troll spat them out, but when he breathed in again, the wasps got sucked back down his throat. Choking anew, the troll waved his arms about, slashing the air and smacking Ren, who was just attempting to make a landing. The little bird, new to flying, careened through the air, finally spiraling to earth like a maple key.

The giant staggered to his feet, sending Boots tumbling all the way to the ground.

"I have a stomachache!" the troll roared. "And a sore foot! And it's all your fault!" Rage-filled and wheezing, he stamped about, crushing anything that happened to be underfoot, which at any moment could include the youngers.

While they scrambled to avoid his feet, the troll himself was so thoroughly occupied trying to step on them that he failed to notice something very important. Dawn was breaking, and the unwary ogre was positioned so he was facing directly into—

"*Hold it right there,*" my companion with multiple heads interrupts me in the middle of my sentence. "*I have a feeling I know how this is going to turn out.*"

"*Do you?*" I ask.

"*Badly for the troll,*" he said, shaking three of his four shaggy heads. The others nod solemnly.

"*He was not the brightest of our lot,*" says one of the heads.

"*The . . . troll . . . he was a friend of yours?*" I ask.

"*Distant cousin.*"

My companions, trolls themselves, hang their heads in remembrance of their relative.

"*Another one gone,*" old graybeard says. "*Before his time. What will happen when we die? Which eventually all must do, whether we misjudge the sunrise and are turned to stone or whether we get so very old we become part of the mountains. Who will carry on after us?*"

"We will have become extinct," says a small one with a voice like a mouse stuck in a silverware drawer.

There is a long silence during which they—and I—contemplate a world without them.

"One more kingdom gone from this Earth," says graybeard.

"Many kingdoms lost. Each one contributed something, and so the Earth is a little less than it was. A little bit quieter," says the four-headed one. His other heads continue the litany of extinctions:

"We are already missing the tiger's growl,

the elephant's trumpet,

the whale's song,

the loon's yodel,

the chest-thumping of gorillas,

the piccolo solos of so many songbirds

the whisper of monarch wings

and on and on . . .

Who will be left to fear the thunderous tread of the troll? Who will miss it if it is gone from the Earth?"

"When you're gone, tell me, what will be lost?" I ask.

The biggest head on the oldest troll turns toward me, firelight flickering in his dark eyes. "Ancient wisdom," he says. "We know the history of the world. And all that has transpired since the dawn of time. That is our burden. But also our pleasure."

"Both a burden and a pleasure?" I ask, wondering.

"Aye," he says, and all the heads in the circle nod in agreement.

"So much wisdom has been lost," says graybeard. "Whales, for instance, *always used to spout off brilliant solutions for knotty worldwide problems, but humans didn't even bother to learn the whales' language before they finished off the species. Now they're gone."*

"So . . . without you," I say, *beginning to realize what is at stake,* "we lose our history. Our knowledge of times past. Our old stories."

Again, the heads bob up and down. The bristly hairs of their heads glisten in the firelight, nodding and nodding.

The only sound is the crackling of the fire and the pop and fizz of sparks as they spiral into the dark sky.

"But," I ask, "are there not young ones to take your places? I mean, when you are gone?"

"Ah," *says old graybeard.* "That is a story for another time. Go on with your tale."

"Where were we?" *I wonder.*

"The sun was rising," *the rumbly voiced one says ominously.*

CHAPTER TWENTY-SIX

THINGS DON'T TURN OUT AS WELL AS HOPED

Oh, yes. The unwary troll was facing directly into the rising sun. Stunned by the burst of light, he stopped. The silence of that moment was broken by a crackling noise—the sound of stone being formed. No sooner had the sun's rays fastened on the giant's face than he was turned instantly to stone.

Tag, her comrades, and Blue watched this in astounded silence. One moment the troll was roaring and stomping, and the next he was as unmoving and silent as, well, stone. The newly released birds wheeled and circled overhead. Brilliantly colored feathers drifted down, settling in the many nooks and crannies that had suddenly formed in this new rock formation.

"He is actually quite good-looking in this form," Tag said, pointing out the dark cave that had been the troll's mouth, the jutting nose, and the little pine tree growing out of the top of the rock. "Don't you think?"

All she got in response was a groan from Boots, a moan from Ant, a whimper from Blue, and the saddest little chirp from Ren.

The tiny brown bird was sitting on a rock, breathing hard, one wing spread out at an odd angle.

"Are you okay?" Tag said, reaching toward the little bird. Ren hopped a few inches away, dragging one wing. "Oh no! Is it a broken wing?" Tag exclaimed, then turned to Boots and Ant. Both of them were slumped against the boulders. "What's the matter with you two?" she asked.

Ant clutched at his stomach. "Belly . . . ache . . ." he groaned.

"Boots?" Tag said.

Boots swayed on his feet, then toppled into her. That's when she saw his oddly misshapen arm.

Tag's stomach lurched. "Oh, no!" she said. "We need help! We need so much help!" But where could she find help in this land of trolls and talking stumps and boats that were maybe not boats? She didn't know, but she'd have to try.

While she made a sling for Boots's arm out of the last

remaining shred of cloth in the rucksack, she called for the dog.

"Blue Tooth! Blue!" she sang out.

A scratching noise caught Tag's attention. She followed the sound to find the little dog digging away at the dirt behind a rock, as if she wanted to hide under it. "What's going on, Blue?" she said. "Is something wrong with you, too?"

The pup just flopped down on the ground and stared up at her with an inscrutable look.

Tag made a slow, sad circle, looking at all her companions—Blue, panting in a hole in the dirt, Ren with one pitiful, probably broken wing, Ant on the ground, groaning, and Boots leaning on the rock that used to be the troll, moaning. Where could they go to get help? An even bigger question: *How* could they go anywhere? It seemed quite impossible. On top of everything else, it had started to snow.

"We've done other impossible things," Tag said to herself. "We can do this."

So she got to work. She constructed a little nest in Ant's antlers and settled Ren gently inside. She emptied the rucksack of the leftovers from the eating contest, slid the still-damp book of fairy tales back into it, and then tucked Blue inside. Then she hoisted Ant and Boots up, leaning one on each side of her.

Now, she thought, *where*? Where could they go to get help?

As she pondered this, a path appeared where she had not previously noticed one. And was it her imagination or were the trees urging her along, gesturing to her with every branch to follow the path, every leaf pointing the way? Even the wind was behind them, seeming to push the youngers along. The birds Boots had freed flew on ahead, pausing to wait for the travelers, then flying again as if urging them onward along this path.

The birds were the only splotches of color in the otherwise drab forest they had entered. Under a coating of snow, the trees were gray, the bark peeling away, their spindly branches draped with the white-green lichen called old man's beard.

But through the falling snow flashed red, blue, yellow—cardinal, jay, goldfinch. The glossy raven flew high above them all, its tether still dangling from one leg.

When Tag took her eye off the sky, it was only to see that Ant had crumpled and plopped down in the snow. Boots, whose face had turned ashy gray, said, "I can't go on."

"We *have* to go on!" Tag said. "We can't stop!"

"Can't," Boots said, slithering out of her grasp and slumping to the ground next to Ant.

Just as Tag was about to collapse in the snow with the others, the wind picked up, rattling the branches and making something creak and groan: a gray wooden sign swinging from a tree branch.

CHAPTER TWENTY-SEVEN
HELP IS FOUND

T ag had to stand on tiptoes and squint to read the lichen-spotted sign:

> Third Sister Office of
> eNCHANTMENT
> AND BEWITCHMENt,
> curse and spell Consultations
> and REVERSALS.
> Plus first aid.

Beyond the sign, a tiny cottage came into view, its siding weathered to gray and so like the surrounding trees, they might have walked right past it if the wind hadn't picked up just then, making the sign squeak.

Tag managed to roust Ant and Boots, promising them that they had only to go a few more steps. Blue wiggled inside the rucksack, and together they all approached the small house.

She rang the bell and waited, expecting whoever came to the door to be just as gray and lichen-covered as everything else.

The woman who opened the door was strangely treelike but very much alive. Her hair was the vivid green of young leaves, coiled on top of her head like a fiddlehead fern, and her face was the variegated color of tree bark. Oddest of all was that her eyes reminded Tag of the knothole at home—like little windows to another world.

The tree-woman beckoned the travelers in as if she'd been expecting them.

Tag felt a little spark of hope flare in her heart.

"Tell me everything," the woman said, "starting with your names."

Tag told her their names, and the woman said that they should call her Nordri.

"My companions need help," Tag said, and the whole story poured out of her, how they'd all been hurt or bewitched. Or both. Ren was a bird but wasn't supposed to be. And now the poor thing had a broken wing. Ant had a terrible stomachache. "Oh, and also antlers," Tag added, probably unnecessarily. "Boots . . ." She gestured toward his injured arm.

A whimper from her rucksack reminded her of the pup

inside, and she shrugged off the pack and scooped Blue out of it. "This is Blue Tooth," she said. "She's acting very strangely. I think she might be sick."

"I don't think she's sick exactly," Nordri said. "But she'll be more comfortable here." She set the pup in a blanket-lined basket, then waved at the others to follow her.

The little gray shingled cottage mysteriously seemed to go on and on. Bundles of dried herbs and strings of mushrooms dangled from the ceiling. Dusty books were piled helter-skelter everywhere, forming corridors through which the group meandered until they came to a room with a long table in its center cluttered with jars and vials, mixing bowls, and lots of books. Light from a dirty window illuminated one very large book that stood open on a lectern.

"So many books!" Tag said.

"Not nearly enough," Nordri said.

"Aren't you afraid?"

"Afraid of books?" Nordri asked.

"Afraid to *have* to so many books," Tag explained.

"No," Nordri said. "I should be afraid to be without books. How would you know anything?"

"But aren't you afraid of the Powers-That-Be?"

"I'm more afraid of being ignorant," Nordri said, going to the woodstove upon which a teakettle whistled away. Nordri filled a teapot with herbs, lifted the kettle off the stove, and poured the boiling water into the pot.

Ant and Boots had both collapsed, Ant on a soft-looking couch and Boots into an overstuffed chair. Tag gazed at the books cluttering the table and stacked on floor-to-ceiling shelves. *Disshelvelment,* Ren would have said, Tag thought.

"You must know a lot then," Tag said admiringly, gazing at the books.

"When you get to my age, you do know a lot." Nordri poured the tea into mugs and handed the mugs to Ant and Boots. "Yet there's always more to know somehow. For one thing, it takes a lot to stay ahead of the creatures on this side of the border. It's not that they're so smart, but they're wily." She stopped to command Boots and Ant to "Drink that!"

They did as they were told.

"Trolls, for instance," she continued, "have no scruples or morals, and that makes them dangerous. Unpredictable. On top of that, they are very strong. And have magic powers."

"We noticed," Tag said, lifting Ren out of the nest in the antlers and setting the little bird on the table. "A troll turned our friend into a bird. Can you help?"

Nordri examined each of those who were injured. "Some of this is just basic first aid. The broken arm. The broken wing. But the other things depend on how long it's been since the enchantment." She sniffed at Boots, Ant, and Ren. "These have that new-spell smell."

Tag took a sniff, but all she could smell were herbs and musty books. "So you can cure them?"

"First things first," Nordri said, turning to Boots. With a quick, decisive movement, she set the bone in his arm.

Of course, Boots let out a horrendous scream, whereupon a whole cave's worth of bats flew out of his mouth.

"Did my sister do that?" Nordri said, eyeing the bats swooping among the rafters.

Tag nodded.

"That's a favorite of hers. Something can be done for it, but it might take a while. Austri never does anything in a straightforward way. It can take some time to untangle her spells." She fixed a splint on Boots's arm and began wrapping it. "I don't suppose she sent a saucepan along with you?"

"Why, yes!" Tag exclaimed, running back to the rucksack to get it. When she returned, Nordri was finishing up wrapping Boots's arm.

"This one," Nordri pointed her chin at Ant, "has obviously eaten a lot of food created by magic. That is very hard on the digestion. I'll fix him a tincture, but he'll need a few days to recover."

"What about his, um, antlers?" Tag asked.

"That was Vestri's doing, I suppose," Nordri said. "Well, they'll fall off in due time. They may grow back, of course."

Now, eyeing the little bird on the table, Nordri crossed her arms, then went straight to the big book on the lectern. She settled herself on a creaky stool in front of it and began turning pages.

"When did this happen?" she asked.

Tag tried to calculate how much time had passed since they'd encountered the troll in the silver forest. "Well, time has been a little hard to keep track of . . ." she said, realizing that strangely she had no idea how long their journey had taken so far.

"Hmm. Well, you see," Nordri said, "some enchantments can be reversed. Some can be twisted a little bit, to make them less bad. But in some cases, the statute of limitations has run out."

"Statue of limitations?"

"Not statue, *statute*. At some point, spells can no longer be undone—and then they just become what is. They become reality and have nothing to do with magic anymore."

"Like what?"

"Let's see . . . Frogs, for instance," she said. "Originally, all frogs were bewitched princes, and some of them found a princess willing to kiss them or throw them against a wall or whatever was required to break the spell, but many didn't have such luck and remained frogs. All the frogs you see today are the descendants of princes and a few bewitched princesses as well. And nowadays they are frogs for good. You can kiss them all you want, but they'll just stay frogs. Although it is wise to remember that they descend from royal lineage."

"What other things started out a spell that became reality?"

"Well, for one thing, greed," Nordri said. "That's a bad one. Nobody has been able—or willing—to break that spell. Now you see it everywhere, greed. One of those things that has multiplied without any effort. It isn't even a spell anymore. It just—I don't know—floats about in the air and people seem to catch it. Like a virus."

"Nothing can be done about it?"

Nordri clucked her tongue. Tapped a twiglike finger on the page, considering.

"The reason I'm asking," Tag said, "is because I wonder if this whole thing with the wind taking youngers is at least partly—or maybe wholly—caused by greed. I mean, that is," she tried to collect her thoughts. "Our community seems to—or the Powers-That-Be—or, well, olders in general seem to value the silver leaves that come when youngers are windswept more than they value us youngers."

Nordri turned her soft, brown eyes on Tag, and Tag couldn't help but peer into them, wondering what wonders lay behind. "You are smart to see right to the root of the problem," Nordri said, "but you need to set that aside for the time being. I have to remind you, young lady, that right now you have less than the amount of time you need to rescue the windswepts."

"How do you know that?"

"Come with me." Nordri led Tag outside, where they climbed a hill to a little promontory where the mountains were visible. Their peaks and slopes were turning a bright, unnatural shade of blue. Even the clouds that clung to their sides were tinged blue.

"That is not good," Nordri muttered.

"What does it mean?"

Nordri turned to Tag, all her brightness seeming to dim. "It means you'll get there too late or never at all."

"Everybody keeps saying that, but what does it *mean*?" Tag asked. "I mean, 'too late' for what?"

Nordri led Tag down the path and back into the cottage while telling her how it was that trolls, ogres, giants, and other large nonhuman troublemakers had, over time, been pushed to the brink of extinction. "It takes them many hundreds of years to reproduce, so building up their numbers is slow," she said. "But they discovered that they could create troll-like trolls and ogre-like ogres out of susceptible humans. Children aren't any more susceptible than grown-ups, but for a troll, a human life is like a wisp of smoke, ephemeral, hardly worth mentioning, so it isn't worth spending the time on grown-ups. The younger they are, the longer they can serve the trolls' interests. Plus, children are easier to carry away on the wind."

"Children? What is that?"

"Oh, my dear!" Nordri's eyes filled with tears, which she swiped away before saying, "You should have had a childhood, but it was denied—locked in your homes and kept away from other children. And now you are already in a place between childhood and adulthood. It is its own kingdom in a way, a kind of in-between kingdom. Quite a remarkable place, but one where you cannot dwell for long."

Tag wanted to consider this, but she knew she had to stay focused on the most urgent problem. "But you've been telling me that our siblings are being made into trolls? We have to save them!"

"It is already too late," Nordri said. "At least for some. After seven years, the enchantment becomes complete and at that point cannot be undone."

"Seven years?" Tag gasped. It had been seven years since her sisters had been windswept. Maybe *exactly* seven years. There'd been mums in the garden, and falling leaves, and her sisters had woven purple asters in their hair. It had been fall, seven years ago. "It can't be!" she cried.

Nordri nodded sadly while filling the saucepan with water.

"But we can still get there, can't we? If we hurry?"

"No," Nordri said, setting the saucepan on the hot woodstove. "Even if you hurry. And your friends are in no condition to go anywhere."

Tag felt like her legs would give out. All this long journey and all their struggles and now they really were going to fail. Like everyone else who had tried.

"And yet . . ." Nordri said, crumbling a few herbs into the pot. "Perhaps . . . maybe . . ."

Tag's heart gave a little thumpity-thump, as if waking up. "And yet . . . perhaps maybe . . . what?"

"You could get the wind to take you!" Nordri exclaimed.

"The wind?" Tag said. "You mean like the way it took our siblings?" Now her heart stood still, as if it was sorry it had thumpity-thumped. "You mean we should have just let the wind take us when it tried to?"

"Oh, no, then you likely would have ended up like all the other children who have been windswept. All of the things you've learned along the way, and all the things you've done along the way—particularly the *impossible* things—will help you. Because things will only get a whole lot more impossible."

"But . . ." Tag said, "the others—Ren, Boots, and even Ant—they're the ones who did all the difficult things. I really just tagged along."

"Well, I'm sure that's not *all* you did," Nordri said. "But you see, they have fulfilled their destinies. Ren's bold wrath kept you from being immediately devoured by the troll and showed you all how to stand up to those bullies; every time a tree needed to be climbed and especially when enchanted birds needed to be released, who could have done that but Boots? And who but Ant could have challenged the troll to an eating match? They have fulfilled their destinies. You have yet to fulfill yours."

"But, still . . . the wind?" she said. "The wind seems to hate us!"

"How can you say that! It's been helping you all along!" Nordri exclaimed.

"Helping us?"

"Can't you think of any times the wind helped you?"

Tag dug around in her memory and realized that she needn't dig very far. "Well, the wind made your sign squeak so I noticed it. Otherwise, I might never have found you."

"Yes?"

"And in sort of the same way, the wind rattled the birch bark at your sister's cottage when we needed a way to carry the goat milk. But, on the other hand, it made the lake so wavy that it capsized our boat."

"And then it must have also blown you to shore. Otherwise, you wouldn't be here."

"I suppose."

"And how did you eat this whole time?" Nordri asked.

"We had a magic tablecloth," Tag said. "When we said, 'Cloth, spread thyself,' the branches would shake fruit or nuts onto the tablecloth."

"And what shook the branches?"

"Well . . . I suppose it was the wind," Tag said. "But still, on our whole journey, the wind has been pushing us *away* from the mountains!"

"That is because, my dear, it was pushing you *here*," Nordri said, untying a leather string from around her wrist. "There really is only one way for you to get to the Troll Mountains." She handed the string to Tag.

"What is this?" Tag asked.

"That," Nordri said, "will get you to the Troll Mountains—and back again."

"This?" Tag said. It was just a simple leather string, knotted three times.

"Untie this knot," Nordri said, pointing to the bottom knot as it hung from Tag's hand, "and it will bring you a steady breeze. Untie this one"—she tapped the middle knot—"and it will bring you a stiff gale. Untie *this* one"—

she tapped the knot at the top—"and get ready for a ride to the mountains."

"So, someone could still get there in time, after all? It isn't impossible?"

"I didn't say that!" Nordri said. "No, it's still too late. And it's still impossible."

"Then what is the point?" Tag flung up her arms in frustration.

"Sometimes you have to carry on as if you don't know it's too late and that what you need to do is impossible. Haven't you learned that by now?" Nordri guided Tag toward the door. "And now you must go. You really have no more time to dawdle."

Tag did not feel as if she'd been dawdling, but she followed Nordri toward the door, protesting the whole way.

"Can I at least say goodbye to my friends?" she pleaded.

"No."

"Oh, but let me get my rucksack." Tag tried to wiggle past Nordri to go back inside.

But Nordri was not budging. "You don't need it."

"I'm too afraid! Will you come with me?" Tag begged. "Please?"

"Some things you must do by yourself," Nordri said, pushing Tag out the door. "And this is one of them."

CHAPTER TWENTY-EIGHT
CALLING THE WIND

Tag had spent her whole life and most of this journey hiding from the wind. Now she was going to go out and call it to her?

She looked longingly back toward the cottage. From this vantage point, she could just make out a square of warm yellow light from a window. The smell of woodsmoke mixed with the scent of rich broth flavored with healing herbs drifted over to her. The urge to run back to that light and warmth and friendship was almost more than she could bear.

Friends, Tag thought. Yes, they really were her friends. They'd been through a lot together. They had helped her. And now it was her turn to help them. If only she knew what that would mean! But she supposed you didn't always know what you'd be called on to do for your friends.

She walked slowly back to the promontory and faced the distant mountains. They loomed so close, it felt as if she could reach out her hand and touch them. Yet Nordri said they were so very far away, the only way to reach them was to have the wind take her there. It seemed quiet, as if the wind were away on business, occupied elsewhere. Far away, maybe. But when Tag looked up at a handful of tall pines, there it was, pushing at the treetops, while the boughs hissed and whispered, annoyed.

A puff of wind billowed her shirt and lifted her hair, as if toying with it. A few snowflakes danced tauntingly in the air. Leaves stirred at her feet, then swirled around her legs.

This wind is not strong enough to take me anywhere, she thought.

Clutching the leather string in her hand, she took a deep breath and loosened the first knot.

With a sudden *whoosh*, the boughs bent and the wind rushed out of the treetops and swirled around her, rattling branches and sending leaves pirouetting at her feet. Like a bully, it slapped the back of her head, gave her a shove, tugged at her sleeve.

This wind is not serious enough to take me anywhere, she thought.

She loosened the second knot.

This time the wind came with a roar. It whipped her hair around her face, twisted her trousers about her legs, pressed tears from her eyes, and nearly, *nearly* lifted her off her feet. But not quite.

This wind is not fierce enough, she thought.

She was not at all sure she wanted to untie the third knot, but she knew that's what she would have to do.

I am as strong and fierce as the wind, she told herself, untying the final knot.

And then it arrived. The *real* wind. It rearranged everything in its path, as if it had never liked any of it—never liked those trees—blow them down! Never liked that shed roof—take it away! Never liked all those leaves on the branches—tear them off! Never liked the sheets hanging on the line, that tarp on the woodpile, those wind chimes—away with them all!

And then the wind turned its attention to Tag and came at her in a wild rush, ready to rid the Earth of her as well. Just before it reached her, it hesitated, as if meeting its match. As if waiting for a command.

"Take me to the windswepts," she said in a voice as clear as mountain air.

The wind spun and twisted, a dark, whirling tornado that seemed to suck everything into its embrace—bits of fluff, shards of bark, shreds of lichen, pine needles, bird feathers, animal dander, the light itself, the very air. Bruised and battered by its pummeling, Tag felt the wind tugging at her, too. At the same time, her feet clung to the earth.

If she was to catch a ride, she would have to give in and let the wind sweep her away. She closed her eyes, stood on tiptoe, and raised her arms like a toddler ready to be lifted into a parent's arms. And then she felt her feet peel away from the ground, her toes last to leave. She hovered for the briefest of moments and then was swept and swirled away so fast it felt as if she and the wind would reach all the ends of the earth at once.

They went skimming over dark valleys and glittering blue rivers; deep forests of great, moss-draped trees; oceans rolling with white caps; woodlands teeming with life; and orchards humming with bees. The trees seemed to hold her aloft as she and the wind tore along, their branches like arms, sending her on her way.

On they went, now whistling over barren mountainsides, strangely silent meadows, acres of concrete, empty cities of glittering metal. Over places where hills had been torn away and huge pits had been left in the earth, where oily slicks floated on waterways and islands of plastic drifted in the ocean. These were remnants of the Other Times.

She saw how the earth was trying to heal itself and where it had not been allowed to. She saw the work that had begun and the work that remained.

She saw all that was good and hopeful and all that was not. She knew she, too, was a part of the whole vast world and all its complexity. Good and bad. Damaged and whole.

At last the wind was so out of breath it could scarce bring
out a puff, and finally it set her down on her feet. Ahead
of her, still across a plain but no longer in the distant
horizon, loomed the mountains. She set off toward them.

There was one thing she didn't notice until just after
sunset, when they were illuminated by the pale twilight:
A row of foothills stood between her and the mountains.

Tag groaned. There were *hills* that had to be negotiated
before reaching the mountains? It would be quite dark by
the time she reached them—which would make it even
harder. She quickened her pace.

But the closer she got to the hills, the more she began to
wonder. What, exactly, were these high, strangely rounded
shapes? And was it a trick of the waning light that they
seemed to be . . . moving? *Toward* her?

CHAPTER TWENTY-NINE
THE HILL-BEINGS

Even through the twilit gloom, it was clear the hills were drawing closer, each plodding step echoing like thunder while lightning crackled behind and between them.

Tag could have turned and run, but between the hulking forms she could see the mountains, lit an eerie blue from the nearly constant pulse of lightning.

The hill-beings kept coming, even though they seemed to be composed of rock and mud and moss and vines, all entangled with sparkling shards of glass and glittering ribbons of plastic. Or maybe they were made of trash into which bark, ferns, moss, and vines had become entangled. It was hard to tell.

"Well," she muttered to herself, "I've never been afraid of hills. Now that I've faced the wind, which I've always been afraid of, I reckon I can face a few hills!"

And so they marched up to each other—Tag and the hills. And as the hill-beings encircled and surrounded her, she recognized them for what they were: trolls.

Very large trolls. There was no way around them, no way through, nor, looking up at their craggy torsos, did she think she could climb over them. Some of them had several heads, and each head possessed one, two, or three eyes, and a slobbering mouth filled with sharp teeth, fangs, or even tusks.

"An intruder!" slobbered the largest of these beings. "You know what we do with intruders, don't you?"

"Show them around? Invite them for a nice meal?" Tag suggested.

"We invite them to *be* a nice meal," one of the giants said, dripping drool as his hand swooped down in an attempt to catch her.

The oldest-looking hill-being with a long beard stopped him. "Tell us, little one," he said. "Tell us who you are and what is your purpose here?"

Tag thought for a moment. She could hardly say, *I am Tag. Short for Tagalong. My real name is Hyacinth. Thirteen and a half years old. I'm here to rescue the windswepts.* She should make herself seem more heroic. So she said, in her strong-as-wind voice, "I am Princess Tagalong Handmedown. I come from the Kingdom of Childhood to demand the release of the windswepts."

"Oh, my!" said the one who seemed to have the most heads—it was hard to tell in the dark. "Well, aren't we impressed, Miss Tagalong Handmedown. I mean, Your Majesty."

The trolls made a show of bowing before her, then threw back their dozens of heads and laughed. Big, slobbery, spit-spraying guffaws.

The old graybeard stepped forward to speak. "Tell us how you came here, and how have you succeeded where so many others have failed?"

"I will tell you," Tag told them. "But first you must release your captives."

"Captives?" said the biggest head of the many-headed one. "We have no captives. If you mean our guests who were brought here by the wind, they are free to come and go as they please. But they do not wish to go. They wish to stay."

"I demand to see them," Tag said.

"You are very demanding for a scrawny, featherless nestling," another one of the troll's heads grumbled, while the others mumbled agreement.

"I remind you that where all others have failed, I have succeeded," Tag answered. "Maybe I am not as much of a featherless nestling as you think."

"We are amused," said one with the voice like thunder. "This could be an entertainment. We'll give you one chance to rescue your dear ones, little squeak."

"All you have to do is find them!" said the one with the wheezy voice who seemed to be made primarily of dead sticks.

"Since you don't know your way around our abode, we'll give you a solid head start. We want to be fair."

"Aye, fair," they all said together. Their laughter, if you could call it that, was a strange collection of grumbling chortles, snorts, and hiccuping sneezes.

"If you can find those you seek, you can try as you might to set them free. But you will find it is impossible."

"Off you go!" said graybeard, gesturing to the mountains. "Time is ticking away. When we find you, you must tell your story, and if it does not keep us entertained, well . . . maybe you'll be tastier and more filling than you look."

—○—

Tag stood for a moment, staring at the mountains. Mountain after dark and forbidding mountain rolled away into the misty distance. One could be lost in them for months, she thought. In the fairy tales, the heroes just somehow wandered into the right mountain where the princesses were held captive. How did they know? How would she ever find the right one?

Sometimes you have to go on as if you didn't know the task was impossible. She remembered Nordri saying something like that. And as she stepped forward, a sound caught her attention: the silken flapping of bird wings. She looked up to see that big, black raven circling in the sky above her, its head tilted with one gemlike eye trained on her.

The raven flew on, then returned, swooping overhead. Where the bird led, she followed, until it banked around a mountainside and disappeared.

As Tag came around the mountain, she saw a great gash in the side of it. Not so much a doorway as a yawning crevasse. On the ledge above the opening perched the raven. It paused to peck at the string or piece of twine tied to its leg, then down it swooped and disappeared into the mountain!

Once again, Tag followed.

Once her eyes had adjusted to the gloom, Tag saw she was standing in a large cave lit with smoky torches. Passageways stretched away in all directions, with damp and dripping walls and stone stairways slimy with mold and algae.

She started down one corridor, thought better of it, and tried another. How could she know which way to go?

A quiet croak made her look up, then trace the movement of the bird, dark as a shadow as it flapped down a tunnellike corridor, then another, then another. Down and down, deeper and deeper into the mountain she went, following the bird.

In every troll or giant or ogre story she'd read, their lairs were lined with copper or filled with treasures: golden spinning wheels, magic harps, piles of silver. There were swords and elixirs and places to hide. There was the giant's friendly wife or robust princesses who'd give advice and hide you when the time came.

So far, there were none of these things. Just the dark, damp, cold stone interior of a mountain and its echoey passageways, large banquet halls, and small nooks and crannies.

Would she find her sisters sitting at spinning wheels, making copper thread? Or picking lentils out of the ashes? Or sweeping up loose gems and gold coins? If she did, she would say to them, "It's certainly a surprise seeing you actually doing chores for a change!"

She imagined the admiring looks her sisters would give her. *She* would be the hero. She would save *them*.

———

Ahead, she made out glimmers of light, little sparkles and twinklings, blinks and flashes. At last, she thought, she had come to the piles of gold and silver likely to be found in a troll's lair. But as she rounded the corner and entered an immense chamber, she saw that what was sparkling and glinting in the smoky light of the torches were piles of broken glass and shards of plastic. The walls were covered with or were maybe *made* of trash: plastic packaging, plastic straws, plastic toothbrushes, toys and more toys, doodads and knick-knacks, and a mountain of plastic bags. Millions of tiny plastic particles caught the light, sparkling like mica.

The raven retreated, tucking its head under its wing as if it couldn't bear to look. But Tag looked. There was enough light to see that among all these things there were people—or at least what once *were* people. Their hair was long, unkempt, and dirty. In fact, the accumulated dirt was so deep that small plants and mushrooms sprouted from their hair and ears, along with threads of dental floss, twist ties, and candy wrappers. Their clothes were ragged and filthy and, in some cases, overgrown with moss or fungi. You could still see the human in some of them, but others had grown tails and small tusks, and, though still young, their faces were wrinkled and rugged, their skin ridged with patches of bristly hair. Some were still small, but others were growing into giants.

Even so, Tag cried out, in relief and sadness, for although some of them were hardly recognizable as people, she knew she had found the windswepts—those she had come to rescue.

Somewhere in this crowd were Ren's twin, Finn's little brother, Boots's and Ant's siblings. Were her own sisters here? And Finn? She looked and looked but couldn't see them. Or else she couldn't recognize them anymore.

The echo of footsteps could be heard in the distance. The trolls were coming! There was no time to search for her sisters—she had to get the windswepts out *now*!

"Hurry!" she called. "Come with me! Quickly!"

"To where?" someone asked.

"Out of here. Out of the mountain."

"We don't want to go," said one.

"We like it here," said another.

"Here?" Tag glanced around at the dimly lit chamber, at its cold floor, slick with grime. The rotten-egg smell of sulfur permeated everything.

"There are a lot of things here," a pale girl in a dirty shift said. "See?" She pulled a small item from one of the heaps and stared at it, turning it in her hands as it winked and flickered.

"Isn't it beautiful?" the girl whispered, enraptured. She took a deep, inhaling breath, as if taking in the scent of a garden. Tag had to choke down the urge to gag. Still, she couldn't help glancing at the glittering thing in the girl's hand and had to admit: There was something appealing about it.

The thud of heavy footfall and the smell of stinking breath washed down the corridors. The trolls would soon arrive.

"Come with me," Tag pleaded. "Let's go home to our families."

"We don't want to go back to those horrible people where we lived long ago. We prefer to stay here with those who understand us," said a wan little one.

"We don't want to come out in the awful sunlight. We prefer to stay here in the lovely dark," said another, brushing the frayed end of his tail against his face.

"Follow me!" Tag yelled over the beeps and dings and odd little whistles.

Heads came up, eyes turned to her, but something in one of the piles of trash glittered and jingled and all eyes went to it. They clustered around the sparkling thing, staring at it, wanting it. Tag went to see what it was, too. Just out of curiosity, she told herself, but suddenly found herself staring at the glowing object. Then moving to another. And another.

Even though the walls shook with the tremor of the trolls' footfall, she couldn't stop moving from one bright object to the next. The walls and piles of things around her were more beautiful than she'd thought at first. You could imagine that it might be a lovely place to spend your days, among these pretty beings and magical things. The soothing dark and the damp seeping into her bones made her feel like someone else entirely, someone stronger, more powerful, more cunning . . . Why had she ever wanted to be anyone else? Or anywhere else? Perhaps she would like to—

Her thoughts were interrupted by a deep, gurgling croak. Tag's eyes flicked toward the sound. A big black bird she vaguely remembered was clinging to a moldy chandelier above her, tugging at something that dangled from its leg.

She was about to turn back to the splendor around her when the raven managed to loosen the old tether, and down it drifted. Tag watched it curling and uncurling until, as it floated past, she snatched it out of the air. It was, she could see in the flickering torchlight, a ribbon. A blue hair ribbon. It seemed to tug at her memory. It meant something. It was from long ago and far away, from another time and place . . . when once upon a time she had lived in a house with sisters. The ribbon had belonged to one of them. But then Tag had given it away . . . to . . .

"Finn?" she said, looking up at the bird. "Is that you?"

The bird made a soft, almost purring noise in its throat.

"Finn!" she said again, remembering everything now. She was here to *rescue* Finn, her sisters, the windswepts, not to *become* one of them!

She clung to the ribbon as if it were keeping her head above an ocean of water. "Please," she managed to squeak out, pleading with the windswepts, "You *have* to come with me! Now!"

But it was too late. She could already hear the breathing of the trolls as they entered the hall.

"So that's where we found you," one of the heads on my four-headed companion says, as I pull packing peanuts out of his hair.

"Defeated," his second head adds, chuckling.

"You tried," says the third head.

"But you failed," says the fourth.

"Well," I tell him as I pull bits of vinyl out of one of his beards, "at least I succeeded in getting all the garbage and trash out of your coats. And you all look pretty good now!"

They do look verdant and healthy, the rocky crags of their fore-heads overhanging with lush forests of young trees and ferns. All garbage-free.

The trolls look themselves over, rather pleased. They twirl their tails, then turn to look at the heap of discarded trash, a pile as big as at least one of them.

"It's sad," old graybeard says, looking at it, "that although we live for hundreds, sometimes even thousands of years, that pile will live longer than any of us."

"Now there," I tell him, "you have spoken truth."

"Hah!" he spits out. "We have found common ground."

There is a momentary lull during which there is only the sound of the crackling fire, the shuffling of hairy feet, and the always heavy breathing of the trolls, as perhaps they contemplate the concept of common ground.

———— ○ ————

Some of the trolls have gotten up and are busy rearranging the coals while others are constructing a little spit upon which I am to be roasted. My story is told, and I am out of ideas. Daylight seems a long way off, and I still have no good idea how to go about getting my sisters and all the other windswepts out of the mountain. Although I guess I could just ask.

"I don't suppose," I say to the trolls, "now that you're planning to roast me anyway, that you'd tell me the secret of how to get the children out of the mountain?"

"There's really only one way," says the tusked one. "And since it's impossible, I guess there's no harm in telling you."

Naturally, it's impossible, I think. What else could it be? "Well, what is it?" I ask.

"You have to weave a rope . . ." says old graybeard.

Well, I know how to do that!

". . . a rope of invisible thread," he goes on, "spun strong as spider's silk, woven of ashes and memories."

That puts a more difficult spin on it.

"But you'll never get the chance to try, anyway," says a troll who is drooling so much, there is a large puddle forming at his feet. "The coals are ready."

Is it too soon to hope for a little glimmer of light in the east—just the pale, almost-light of predawn? Apparently it is, for the sky goes on being as dark as ever, the stars twinkling away like tiny pinpricks in the fabric that separates this world from yet another.

Is this it, then? This is really how the story is going to end? I won't have rescued anybody and I'll be roasted on a spit and eaten for a late-night snack?

"What do you want with all those youngers, anyway?" I ask them. "You can't just go about stealing people to try to turn them into versions of yourself!"

"We can and we have and we will!" says old graybeard.

"Also, technically, we don't steal them. We pay for them," says broken tusk.

"And also, technically, we don't steal them," says the sticks and twigs one. "The wind does. Although to be fair, we control the wind. You're not the only one with a windstring, assuming that's what got you here."

Just to make sure I still have it, I feel in my pocket for the windstring. Still there.

"But, anyway, humans started it," rumbles the thunder-voiced one.

"Started what?"

"Stealing children."

"What? What are you saying?"

"Are you telling us you don't know that humans stole our children long before we started stealing—or, rather, buying—theirs?"

"That can't be true," I say. "You're doing that troll thing where you just make up a story and say that it's true."

"Isn't that what you've been doing?"

"No."

"Humans decided there were too many of us, so they started 'culling,' which is a fancy way of saying, 'stealing our children.' We phylum of trolls, part of the larger kingdom of Giants, Ogres, and Other Large Bullies, should actually qualify for endangered species protection, if such a thing existed anymore. In addition to habitat loss (human caused), overhunting (by humans), and general harassment (also by humans), humans stole almost all of our children. This was their plan to rid the Earth of us. So we had to do something, take matters into our own hands—or risk becoming extinct!" This speech comes from a rather lumpy old fellow who has been silent up until now.

"We've always been either despised or misinterpreted as cute, fuzzy comical cartoon characters, which we are not," says one who is kind of cute and fuzzy, actually.

"I get that," I tell him.

"No one really understands us, you know. We wouldn't have to be so mean, but we are."

"If you don't have to be, why are you?"

"Anger. Like a lot of nonhumans, our kind is nearly extinct."

"I'm sorry," I say, and find myself meaning it. I suppose, even though trolls are sometimes very badly behaved, unpleasant, smelly, and steal youngers, they're probably an important part of some ecosystem or another.

"Does it always have to be about humans?" the troll goes on. "What makes humans so special? Why should human life take precedence over a butterfly's? Or a bird's, say?"

I glance up at the bird I think might be Finn, wondering.

"Why are humans the ones with rights?" says the one with her head under her arm. "Where are our rights? Where are the rights of"—she flings out her free arm—"mountains? Why shouldn't the stars have the right to shine, instead of being blotted out by the lights humans throw up into the sky? And primarily, why don't trolls get any rights?"

"Well . . ." I start to say.

"Well, what?" the troll snaps.

"Well, most people don't even believe you exist!"

"That's what I'm talking about!" the troll howls, wiping her eye with her tail. "Human beings can just decide to not believe in something, and then—poof—it's like it disappears! It doesn't exist as far as they're concerned, so they pay it no more mind. But that doesn't mean it doesn't exist! Garbage, for instance. People kept throwing away things—plastic and more plastic—just throwing it away and then, I suppose, they felt as if it was gone. As if it didn't exist anymore. But here it still is, after all this time, piling up and up and up." She points to the big pile of garbage I had pulled off them.

"What humans do believe," says one of the heads on the four-headed troll, "is that they are more important than any other living being on Earth. What makes them think that?"

I suppose he expects an answer, but I don't have one. As Ren says, in the stories, trolls represent the worst of humankind. Our uncontrolled appetites. Greed. Avarice. Maliciousness. But that is when a troll is in a story and meant to be a metafork. I mean metaphor. Now, here before me, on the far side of the fire, sits a real troll, who looks at me with a dozen sad, brown eyes, like a big, shaggy, many-headed sheepdog. His face in all its weirdness with its tusks and wrinkles; his fur stuck full of greasy foodstuffs. Nonetheless, he registers feelings, and right now, his eyes are pools of sorrow, and every crease in each of his faces tells of hardship.

Have I spent so much time with these trolls that I am starting to see things their way? I am confused, no longer sure of what to do. Yet, I remind myself that I came here to rescue the windswepts from the mountain. I have to stay alive to do that. And the only way I can see to do both of those things is to keep these trolls out until daybreak, when they will turn to stone.

At least that has always been my plan. And now I notice the pale white light that fringes the mountains behind the trolls. Soon the sun will rise—I hope. I just need to keep the trolls talking.

"Enough talk!" says the tusked one. "Time to grill!"

Three of the younger ones get up and lunge at me. They are faster than you'd think for their size. But what they don't know is that I had three older sisters who tried to catch me when it was bedtime or bath time or time for chores, and I developed skills.

"You are as slippery as a bar of soap," Lily used to say. Now I put those slippery skills to use, dodging grasping paws, ducking swinging arms, and evading stomping feet. If I'm lucky, I'll stay out of their grasp just long enough for the sun to rise.

"You're as slippery as soap," says one of the trolls.

I stop in my tracks, and this is my undoing. I'm snatched up and held close to my captor's face.

"Do I know you?" I say slowly, staring at those eyes, the only part of the troll that seems, just at this moment, untroll-like. In fact, there is something in those eyes that is very, very human. And very, very familiar.

Something rustles in my pocket. The ribbon. It chooses this moment to swim out of my jacket pocket, float up into the air, and hover in front of the troll's befuddled face.

To my surprise, there is a flicker in the troll's eyes that at first I take for interest, but maybe it's more than that. Maybe it's recognition.

"Lily?" I ask.

The eyes—now so familiar—flick over my face. Behind her, I pick out two other trolls. "Rose?" I squeak, "Iris?"

Behind them, the hot, red rim of the sun emerges between two mountain peaks.

"Lily . . ." I whisper, looking into her eyes. "The sun is about to rise. You'd better take shelter."

The troll who might be Lily sets me down and she and the other two charge toward the mountain. The other trolls heave themselves up in a kind of slow-motion panic. They begin to lumber toward the opening in the mountain, which they all try to get through at the same time, creating a trollish traffic jam. I dart under their legs and into the mountain.

Down, down, and down I go, farther and farther, dashing around corners, back to the chambers where the windswepts move from one bright object to the next.

It may be too late to save my sisters, but maybe I can save the others. If I can, will I be able to get them out of the mountain with the trolls so close on my heels?

All the way down the cavernous hallway, I think about the rope of invisible thread, spun strong as spider's silk, woven of ashes and memories. And what will I use to weave such a rope? My rucksack was left behind, the book and the clothes with it. All I have left is words.

So words are what I'll use.

<hr />

As I enter the chamber filled with the windswepts, I just start talking. I spin a tale of gleaming white birch trees against a periwinkle sky, of snow-frosted firs and a layer cake of smells, each layer telling of seasons past and seasons coming: damp earth, sun-warmed pine, fallen leaves, fresh snow, young ferns, new green growing things.

<hr />

I tell of windows that let in the sunlight and of tree-climbing brothers— big brothers in big boots. Of tree houses and village council meetings. Of a house holding its breath waiting for the return of its youngers, a house filled with photographs and rooms left untidied and unchanged—still with socks on the floor and a guitar on the bed.

Of loving siblings, grieving parents, broken families waiting, longing for them.

I weave a story of light and dark, of fierce little sisters, brave brothers, intrepid dogs. Of dangerous journeys and friendships found.

I weave a tapestry of words, of the clatter of heels on the stairs, of late-night pillow fights and clouds of feathers in the air like snow. I tell of snow. And rain.

A little light comes into their eyes, a glimmer of something. I start walking backward, pulling them out of the rathole with a rope made of ashes—of what has been lost or never known. Summer twilights filled with screen doors slamming, the shouts of youngers playing outside on grass wet with dew, of windows sliding open, of snow forts and leaf piles.

The three trolls that answer to the names of Iris, Rose, and Lily lean in, listening, so I tell of piano music and the smell of cardamom buns steaming on the kitchen table, of a father in the garden strumming the ukulele, the music and the scent of night-blooming jasmine wending its way into their bedroom windows.

———o———

I tell of a mother pacing the floor in a dress so stiff that it keeps her heart from breaking.

———o———

I weave a rope of memories—of attic stairs that fold down with a clatter, of a window that reveals the world, of dress-up clothes and a forbidden book tucked away in a hidden place, and three girls' heads bowed over that book, whispering the stories to each other as the light streams in through the one small window, stories of kings and princesses, of faraway castles and gloomy woods, of glass slippers and silver forests, enchanted frogs and fearsome, fearsome trolls. Made-up stories that are also somehow very, very true.

Little by little, and one by one, the windswepts turn toward me, my words reaching them, tugging at their hearts.

"Our families need us," I tell them. "Our world needs us."

They move toward me, and I keep talking, telling them of their homes and families waiting for them, imperfect as they may be, but loving them and missing them, and they follow all the way out of the mountain and into the bright light of day.

CHAPTER THIRTY

WHAT HAPPENED THEN

Tag took out the windstring and was surprised to see the knots had retied themselves. Once again, she loosened the knots one at a time, and the wind came and lifted her and all the windswept children aloft— almost gently this time—and carried them to Nordri's house. Like many scary things, it was not as scary the second time.

The trolls who had always been trolls stayed behind, safe inside their mountain hideaway. The trolls who had been children, including Tag's sisters, joined the other windswepts, while above them soared a big raven with its black wings outstretched.

By the time the wind set the children down, the fresh air had served as a kind of strengthening elixir, and their color and youth were returning. Even Tag's sisters had become almost recognizably human, the seven years having been not *quite* used up. The raven circled and circled and finally landed on Nordri's roof and, with some coaxing, came inside.

Thanks to Nordri's care, Ant, Boots, and Ren had all recovered and were back to their normal selves. Ren was not a bird anymore but, like Boots, had one arm in a sling. Ant looked more comfortable without his antlers, although he planned to take them home and mount them on a wall. And Boots was no longer spitting out bugs.

Blue leapt into Tag's arms and licked her face until she couldn't take it, and she set the little dog down again. Blue and the raven went nose to beak, then Blue rolled over on her back, letting the raven scratch her belly with its beak.

"Blue Tooth was not sick, after all," Nordri explained, pulling back a blanket on a basket to reveal seven little puppies. "Apparently she had a boyfriend back home."

Those puppies finished the work of transforming the windswepts back into human children, a job to which puppies are profoundly well suited.

Nordri had to go to her big book to find out if Tag's sisters could be turned all the way human again. "It says here," Nordri read, "that to rid them of their troll-hides, you have to beat them with the twigs of nine new birch brooms, and then rub it off in three tubs of milk; first in a tub of last year's whey, then in sour milk, and then rinsed in a tub of sweet milk." She looked up and over at the trollish sisters who had gotten down on the floor and were playing with the puppies. "Or," Nordri said, "we could just let the puppies work their magic."

As for Finn, he looked more like himself every day, transforming into human form, wings to arms, iridescent feathers to glossy black hair.

When Tag's friends and the windswepts were all recovered enough to finish their journey, Nordri gathered them together and said, "You have all survived something hard, and you have grown stronger because of it. Use this strength to create a new and better life for yourselves and for all the kingdoms and their inhabitants on our one and only Earth."

They said their goodbyes and made their way back to the border.

Along the way, Tag asked Finn, "When you said that each of us had a special talent and that's why you invited us on the quest, what talents were you thinking of? I mean, what did you think was special about me, if you don't mind me asking?"

"What was special about you," Finn said, "was that on that first day when I gave you the invitation, you said yes. You came to the meeting!"

"That's it?"

"All I knew about any of you was that you were willing to say yes to the adventure."

"That's all?"

"But that's big. That's the most important thing. And it turned out you all *did* have something important and unique to bring to the journey."

"I think that was only because you said that we would," Tag admitted. "So we each tried very hard to have there be something special about us."

Finn gave her a crooked little smile, plucked one of his few remaining feathers, and stuck it in her braid. Tag returned the favor by tying the blue ribbon around his unruly hair.

Shortcut was waiting for them with Puff all decked out with piles of chopped wood, ready to go. They crossed the border without incident (the border patrol was glad to see the back of them. "And stay there!" he hollered).

It took a few trips, but Puff proudly ferried them home, where they were welcomed as heroes.

With great joy, families were reunited. Tag's mother greeted her daughters at the garden gate wearing a bright yellow, loosely flowing smock. She embraced each of them in turn, saving the last and longest for her youngest.

The Powers-That-Be were not altogether pleased that the wind no longer brought the silver leaves and an entirely new economic system would have to be devised—and just how was *that* going to work? But that gave them plenty of reason to keep meeting and discussing and forming committees and subcommittees, so perhaps they didn't mind so much, after all.

Children—the term came back into fashion—were allowed to play Outside, and some of the older ones took great pleasure in helping the young ones to build forts in the woods and teaching them how to identify and forage for wild foods.

Boots showed them how to climb trees, and Ant gave them instruction in how to build campfires, and Ren taught them a few handy oaths and curses.

Tag collected the once-forbidden books that had been hidden away in peoples' houses and established a lending library. "It's a start," she said. "These books will help us regain some of our old knowledge. And somehow we'll figure out a way to learn what the trolls know and write it down so we can learn our own history."

Together, Tag and her friends worked to give the children the confidence to do pretty much anything, including impossible things, for there were many more knotty problems left to solve, some of which were undoubtedly impossible.

The wind was only too pleased to lift kites, fill the sails of toy boats, blow insects away, and once in a while, with supervision, take them wherever they wanted to go. It was practice for when they would someday set off to find the stolen troll children and return them to their rightful parents. This was considered an entirely impossible task, and so, of course, they could hardly wait to get started. To prepare for the journey, Tag read from an old and tattered book, full of holes, which everyone helped to fill in with their imaginations.

AUTHOR'S NOTE

When I was a kid, my father used to read aloud in Norwegian from an old and tattered book of fairy tales, translating into English as he went along. Since I didn't understand a word of Norwegian, the reading parts served as musical interludes during which I, like Tag, filled in the spaces of these sparely told tales with my own images of moss-draped trees, shadowy forests, and mountainous trolls.

Perhaps because of this long, slow percolation of the tale-telling—the reading, then translating, reading, then translating—these stories seem to have seeped into my bones and, like calcium or some other essential mineral, have become part of who I am.

Tales from the north seemed fitting for a group of youngers who, on their journey, travel north and yet farther north. The young people in this story are not from those northern European cultures, nor from any other of our time. They are "in another kingdom, in another time," as the fairy tales say. Like our own time, theirs has made some positive strides, but also like our own, theirs has neglected to learn from its past or consider its children's future.

"The Three Princesses in the Mountain Blue" is the tale that most directly inspired this story, but I freely borrowed from many others, also Norwegian, including "The Ash Lad Who Had an Eating Match with a Troll,"

"The Boys Who Met the Trolls in the Hedal Woods," "Kari Woodenskirt," and others.

In defiance of the stereotype of helpless maidens being rescued by handsome princes, Scandinavian stories are just as likely to feature tenacious and resourceful girls rescuing enchanted princes, their brothers, themselves, or each other—or giving detailed instructions to their rescuers on how to rescue them. Several such stories are marked with an asterisk on the list that follows.

I didn't restrict my pillaging to Norwegian tales—bits and pieces from German, French, Russian, British, and Irish stories are represented as well. Carrying water in a sieve, a magic tablecloth, a forest of silver, and nasty critters falling from a rascal's mouth are motifs that can be found in tales from around the world.

I'm sure I have forgotten or perhaps don't even *know* all the stories I've "borrowed" from. In fact, it was not until I was paging through anthologies while writing this note that I noticed the tale "The Blue Ribbon" (Norwegian). In it, a boy finds a blue ribbon (or belt in some tellings) that bestows on him such strength that he feels he "could lift the whole mountain." In my story, the blue ribbon (where did *that* come from? I wondered when it first floated away from Tag's hand) bestows no such physical strength but encourages Tag to keep moving ahead, a kind of strength of its own.

Some things, like the idea of an enchanted string capable of conjuring the wind, are not just folklore. Over the course of several centuries, becalmed sailors really did purchase these magical strings from Sami or Finnish wind wizards whose proximity to the source of northern gales presumably gave them special knowledge about how to control them.

Ever since they were collected from storytellers and set down on paper, fairy tales have drawn criticism and even, like some of their characters, have suffered banishment. It's true that fairy tales are often weird, disturbing, gruesome, absurd, even offensive. In fact, reflective of life. As Wilhelm Grimm pointed out to those who wanted to expunge those aspects from the Grimms tales, "You can fool yourself into thinking that what can be removed from a book can also be removed from real life."

I am grateful to all the tale-tellers who kept and continue to keep these tales alive in all their weirdness. These stories remind us that in a sometimes dark and scary world, if we can pluck up our courage, act with compassion toward others, and accept the advice and gifts that are offered, we can overcome all obstacles, even impossible ones, and just maybe, against all odds, things will turn out all right.

TALES REFERENCED AND BORROWED FROM

Norwegian:

* *The Three Princesses in the Mountain Blue*

The Ash Lad Who Had an Eating Match with a Troll

* *Kari Stave-Skirt* (or *Woodenskirt*)

The Boys Who Met the Trolls in the Hedal Woods (a story Tag tells)

The Parson and the Sexton (the more footsteps you take . . . the sun rises in the east and sets in the west, therefore . . .)

* *The Three Sisters Who Were Taken into the Mountain*

The Companion (the recipe for turning a troll back into a human girl again)

* *White Bear, King Valemon* (magic tablecloth)

* *East of the Sun, West of the Moon* (riding on the winds)

* *The Twelve Wild Ducks*

The Lad Who Went to the North Wind (conversing with the wind, also a magic tablecloth)

* *Soria Moria*

Butterball (the troll who carries her head under her arm)

The Blue Ribbon

---

* Stories in which girls rescue boys, their sisters, brothers, themselves, or substantially participate in their own rescues.

Other:

Sleeping Beauty (a story Tag tells)

The Frog King (a story Tag tells—the version with the odd little Iron Heinrich tale at the end)

Rapunzel

* *Rumplestiltskin*

Little Red Riding Hood

* *Vasilisa the Brave*

Snow White

Jack and the Beanstalk

BIBLIOGRAPHY

Asbjørnsen, Peter Christen, and Jørgen Engebretsen Moe. *Norske folke-eventyr*. Oslo: Gyldendal Norsk Forlag, 1932.

———. *Norwegian Folktales*. Trans. Pat Shaw and Carl Norman. New York: Pantheon, 1982.

———. *The Complete and Original Norwegian Folktales of Asbjørnsen and Moe*. Trans. Tiina Nunnally. Minneapolis: University of Minnesota Press, 2019.

Boose, Claire, ed. *Scandinavian Folk and Fairy Tales*. New York: Avenel, 1984.

Dasent, George Webbe, trans. *East O' the Sun and West O' the Moon: 59 Norwegian Folk Tales*. New York: Dover, 1970.

D'Aulaire, Ingri. *D'Aulaire's Book of Trolls*. New York: New York Review of Books, 2006.

DeBlieu, Jan. *Wind: How the Flow of Air Has Shaped Life, Myth, and the Land*. Boston: Houghton Mifflin, 1998.

Zipes, Jack, ed. *The Golden Age of Folk and Fairy Tales from the Brothers Grimm to Andrew Lang*. Indianapolis: Hackett, 2013.

Grimm, Jacob, and Wilhelm Grimm. Ed. Maria Tatar. *The Annotated Brothers Grimm*. New York: W. W. Norton, 2004.

———. *The Original Folk and Fairy Tales of the Brothers Grimm* (Complete First Edition). Trans. Jack Zipes. Princeton: Princeton University Press, 2014.

———. *The Complete Fairy Tales of the Brothers Grimm*. Trans. Jack Zipes. New York: Bantam, 1987.

Haviland, Virginia. *Favorite Fairy Tales Told in Russia*. New York: Beech Tree, 1995.

Melville, Herman. *Moby-Dick; or, The Whale*. New York: Penguin, 1992.

Rose, Carol. *Giants, Monsters & Dragons: An Encyclopedia of Folklore, Legend, and Myth*. New York: W. W. Norton, 2000.

Tatar, Maria, trans. *The Annotated Classic Fairy Tales*. New York: W. W. Norton, 2003.

ACKNOWLEDGMENTS

I'd like to thank my readers and re-readers, the bighearted yarn-spinners of Atsokan Island, Mary Casanova, Phyllis Root, Lauren Stringer, Marsha Chall, Anne Ylvisaker, Catherine Friend, Polly Carlson-Voiles, Sheryl Peterson, and Kelly Dupre. And thanks to Catherine Preus for extra scrutiny. Thanks to Jonathan Auxier for saying something kind and generous that gave me the confidence to follow this path into the forest. Thanks, too, to my patient husband, Arno, and son Pasha for input, with an extra migwech to my youngest son, Misha Kahn, who helped set this ball of yarn rolling and who steered me to Armando Veve, who deserves a wheelbarrow full of troll treasure for the fabulous and fantastical art within and without.

Half the kingdom (or at least 15 percent) goes to my agent-wizard Stephen Fraser. And a forest of silver to all the fine folks at Abrams/Amulet who go about their day accomplishing impossible tasks, not the least of which was turning this jumble of sentences into a book: Megan Carlson, Rachael Marks, and Sara Sproull, with a shout-out to Deena Fleming and Chelsea Hunter for the enchanting fairy tale touches throughout. To my brilliant editor, Howard Reeves, thank you.

In light of current events, this seems like a good time to thank my elementary school librarian for not bowing to pressure to remove *Harriet the Spy* from our library. Parents complained, like one in Xenia, Ohio, who worried that the book would teach children to "lie, spy, backtalk, and curse." That stuff I learned from the neighborhood kids. What I learned from *Harriet the Spy* was to love to write.

Lastly, I am grateful to my father for having introduced me to fairy tales, sometimes in the form of tairy fales "for the fiddle loke and biggle tooper peep" and sometimes in Norske, which would always end with

> *Snipp snapp snute, så var eventyret ute.*
> *Snipp snapp snout, now my tale is told out.*